30P

Blith

CW00540224

WITHDRAWN FROM ISLINGTON LIBRARIES

Blithe
Spirit

Noël Coward

Adapted as a novel by

Charles Osborne

Methuen

Published by Methuen 2004

1 3 5 7 9 10 8 6 4 2

Methuen Publishing Ltd
215 Vauxhall Bridge Road
London SW1V 1EJ
www.methuen.co.uk

Blithe Spirit copyright © 1942 by the Estate of the late Noël Coward

Novelisation copyright © 2004 by Charles Osborne

ISBN 0 413 77245 4

Methuen Publishing Limited Reg. No. 3543167

A CIP catalogue for this title is available from the British Library.

Typeset by SX Composing DTP, Rayleigh, Essex

Printed and bound in Great Britain by
Mackays of Chatham Plc, Chatham, Kent

This book is sold subject to the condition that it shall not,
by way of trade or otherwise, be lent, resold, hired out
or otherwise circulated in any form of binding or cover
other than that in which it is published and without
a similar condition, including this condition, being
imposed on the subsequent purchaser.

To Ken Thomson

ISLINGTON LIBRARIES	
LIBRARY & ACC. No.	
CLASS No.	F
CATG'D	DATE

Chapter

Chapter One

---■---

Southgate Manor, the elegant eighteenth-century home of Charles and Ruth Condomine, set in gently undulating hilly country in the county of Kent, looked especially attractive in the sunlight illuminating its facade at around eleven o'clock on a glorious morning in the summer of 1960. Inside the house, in his study on the first floor, Charles Condomine, an attractive man of about forty, sat at a desk staring moodily at his typewriter. A well-known writer, two of whose novels had become best-sellers, he was currently at work on his latest book, a thriller, a principal character of which was a mentally unbalanced woman who dabbled in the supernatural and who made her living as a professional medium. Charles had worked out the details of his plot satisfactorily, and had already written the first

I

chapter, but now, in chapter two, he had introduced the medium and was having difficulty in bringing her to life convincingly.

After a few moments Charles began to type, muttering the words as he did so. 'When Frau Dosselmann had called for silence, she instructed the five people sitting around the table to place their hands in front of them, with their fingers touching those of the person nearest to them. Then she called –'

He broke off, exclaiming 'No, that's no good', pulled the paper out of the typewriter, screwed it up and threw it across the study. Putting another sheet of paper in the typewriter, he stared at it for a minute or two before trying again. 'Frau Dosselmann considered herself to be a successful medium, but these five people were sceptical of her powers, and she knew she had to –' He broke off again, shook his head despairingly, and went on staring at the page in front of him.

Charles was still sitting motionless some minutes later when his wife Ruth came into the room quietly, walked over to him, and put her arms around him from behind.

'How's it going, my love?' she whispered.

Without looking up at her, Charles replied, 'It's bloody well not going at all. I know what this damned medium has to do, but I just can't find the words. I don't know how she'd express herself. I suppose that's understandable, since I've never known a medium, and –'

'But that's not so, darling, is it?' Ruth reminded him. 'After all, we have a medium only a couple of miles away, in the village. Madame Arcati. We've both spoken to her often.'

'Yes, but only *en passant*, so to speak,' Charles pointed out. 'I know she advertises in the local newspaper that she's a professional medium, but we've never been to one of her bloody seances. We've never even been to her little cottage. We exchanged a few words with her once in the market square, but we've not been to her place and we've never invited her here. If we had, I might have more idea of how she talks, what expressions she uses, and –'

He broke off, paused for a moment, and then got up excitedly, turned to his wife, and exclaimed, 'That's it! We'll invite her here. We can say we've always wanted to know her better, and would like her to come to dinner one evening, and put on a seance for us afterwards. We'd need to invite one or two other people as well, of course –'

'That's a splendid idea, Charles,' Ruth interrupted. 'We could invite our nice local doctor, Dr Bradman, and his wife. We've intended to do so, and this would be an ideal opportunity.'

'Yes, the Bradmans would fit in nicely,' Charles agreed. 'We'd probably have to warn them what we were up to, so that they didn't say the wrong thing, because –'

'Leave it to me,' Ruth declared. 'I'll drop Madame Arcati

3

and the Bradmans a little note, inviting them for – let's make it Saturday week, shall we?'

'Well, I suppose I can put this wretched book on hold until then,' Charles admitted. 'All right, Saturday week, then.' He hugged Ruth and kissed her.

Chapter Two

———

Over the next few days, Charles continued to work on his novel, though in a somewhat desultory fashion, for he had decided not to devote too much mental energy to it until he had had a chance to study Madame Arcati in detail. On the Saturday of the proposed dinner party, he spent the day away from his study, pottering in the garden, and then, early in the evening, after relaxing in a hot bath, he took his time to dress for dinner.

He and Ruth had decided that 'elegant but informal' would be the dress style for the evening, and had informed their guests accordingly. As Charles chose his tie with care, and then donned a loose-fitting velvet smoking jacket, he could hear their new maid Edith scampering about down-stairs. He smiled, shaking his head. Edith was excellent in many ways, but it was proving almost impossible to stop her from doing everything at great speed.

At that moment, Edith, a middle-aged cockney woman wearing both a smart black and white uniform and a permanently anxious expression, was rushing into the comfortably furnished ground-floor living room whose French windows opened onto the garden. She was carrying a large tray of cocktail ingredients which, miraculously, she did not allow to spill or fall from the tray as she raced over to a table near the double doors that led into the dining room. Setting the tray down with a sigh of relief, Edith turned nervously as she heard her employer Ruth Condomine come into the room from the hall that led to the upstairs rooms, as well as to the kitchen and the maid's bedroom in the basement.

Ruth was wearing a pale pink evening gown that was both simple and elegant, her blonde hair tied up away from her elegantly made-up face. She went over to the drinks table and satisfied herself that everything necessary was there. 'That's right, Edith,' she nodded reassuringly to the maid. 'Now you'd better go and fetch the ice bucket.'

'Yes'm,' replied Edith. She turned and was about to run out of the room when Ruth, who was now carefully arranging the various ornaments that stood on the grand piano, stopped her. 'Hold on, Edith,' she called. 'There's no hurry. But did you manage to get the ice cubes out of those little tin trays in the refrigerator?'

'Yes'm,' Edith told her. 'I 'ad a bit of a struggle, though – but it's all right. I managed it.'

'Good. And you filled the little trays up again with water?' Ruth asked.

'Yes'm,' Edith assured her employer. She stood to await any further instructions, but looked prepared to sprint off at the drop of a hat.

'Very good, Edith – you're making giant strides,' Ruth congratulated her, going to the window and arranging the curtain.

'Yes'm,' Edith replied again. She still sounded nervous, perhaps not used to standing still for so long.

Ruth Condomine turned away from the window to address her maid. 'Dr and Mrs Bradman and Madame Arcati are coming to dinner,' she told her. 'Now, Madame Arcati, Mrs Bradman and I will have our coffee in here after dinner, but Mr Condomine and Dr Bradman will stay in the dining room to have theirs, and no doubt some brandy as well.'

When Edith looked somewhat puzzled at this, Ruth said, 'That's what ladies and gentlemen do after dinner. The men stay at the table, while the women leave and go into another room for some private women's talk. Is that quite clear?'

'Yes'm,' was Edith's inevitable response.

Ruth looked at the maid for a moment before continuing, 'And when you're serving dinner, Edith, do please try to remember to do it calmly and methodically.'

Edith gave a little curtsy. 'Yes'm,' she replied.

'As you're not in the Navy, or any of the armed forces as far as I am aware,' Ruth observed somewhat tartly, 'it is unnecessary to do everything at the double. Is that absolutely clear?'

'Yes'm. Very good, 'm,' replied Edith, now sounding more nervous than ever.

Ruth nodded her head. 'Now go and get the ice, Edith,' she instructed, at which, already straining at the leash, Edith started off at top speed.

'Not at a run, Edith. What did I just tell you?' Ruth reminded her sharply. 'A steady pace, please.'

Edith slowed down, uttered another 'Yes'm,' and left the room at a somewhat less frantic pace.

As Ruth Condomine went across to the fireplace, casting a comprehensive glance around the room to check that all was in order, her husband Charles came in from the hall. 'No sign yet of the advancing hordes?' he asked Ruth.

'I don't think three people can be described as hordes, darling,' she replied. 'But no, they're not here yet.'

Charles went across to the cocktail tray. 'Oh dear, no ice,' he observed. 'We're not going teetotal, I hope?'

'The ice is coming,' Ruth assured him. 'I've been trying

8

to discourage Edith from being quite so fleet of foot – it can be awfully dizzy-making for the guests who don't know her – so you mustn't mind if everything is a little slow motion this evening.'

Charles gave a patient sigh. 'I'll believe that when I see it,' he murmured. 'Actually, I would really welcome some slow motion this evening. The last few days since Edith began working here have been extremely agitating. Nothing seems to be going right.' With a puzzled look, he asked Ruth, 'What do you suppose induced our lovely Agnes – a perfect maid – to leave us and go and get married?'

'The reason was becoming increasingly obvious, Charles dear,' his wife pointed out. 'I know we didn't discuss it, but surely you must have noticed.'

'Yes,' Charles agreed. 'I did notice subconsciously, I suppo. e. I was too preoccupied with my novel. But, in any case, nowadays nobody thinks anything of that sort of thing. She could have popped into the local cottage hospital, had the kid, and popped out again, couldn't she?'

'I think her social life would have been seriously under-mined,' said Ruth. 'We may not have minded her being pregnant. But her own friends and acquaintances would have given her a hard time.'

Charles shook his head sadly. 'Well, we'll simply have to keep Edith in the house more,' he observed. 'She won't get into trouble if we don't let her out.' He was about to add something when Edith came back into the room, walking very slowly, and carrying an ice bucket.

Charles and Ruth exchanged a glance of amusement and surprise. 'That's right, Edith,' Ruth congratulated the maid. 'That's splendid. Now, just put it down on the table.'

'Yes'm,' Edith replied as she put the ice bucket on the drinks table which held a vast array of bottles.

Patting the pockets of his jacket, Charles said, 'Edith, I must have left my cigarette case on my dressing table upstairs. Would you get it for me, please?'

'Yes, sir,' Edith responded instantly, dashing quickly out of the room.

'There now!' Charles exclaimed, gesturing helplessly at his wife. 'What on earth are we going to do? She's still at it.'

'No, darling, that's not fair,' said Ruth. 'You took her by surprise. After all, she's still learning. We'll just have to keep working at it. I'm sure she'll improve.'

Charles shook his head helplessly as he went across to the cocktail table, muttering 'I hope you're right.' He surveyed the cocktail ingredients. 'Oh well, I think we each deserve a dry Martini,' he suggested. 'Is that a good idea? You'll have your usual olive in yours and, since I can't make up my mind, I'll have an olive *and* a twist.'

Ruth took a cigarette from a box on the mantelpiece, and lit it, then went across to an armchair and sat. 'Yes, darling,' she replied. 'A Martini now is just what we need. But I think Madame Arcati will want something sweeter.'

Charles nodded. 'I've no doubt she will,' he agreed. 'And it will probably be something we haven't got. Anyway, we'll have this one for ourselves before they all get here.'

Ruth lit her cigarette, and drew on it. 'Oh dear, oh dear,' she murmured.

Charles looked at her anxiously. 'What's the matter, darling?' he asked.

Shaking her head slowly, Ruth replied, 'I have a feeling – I don't know why – but I just have a feeling that this evening's going to be absolutely awful.'

Charles gave her a reassuring smile. 'It'll probably be quite funny,' he admitted, 'but not absolutely awful, I hope. Cheer up, darling.'

Ruth laughed. 'You must promise not to catch my eye,' she warned him, pointing her cigarette at him as she spoke. 'If I giggle – and I'm very likely to – it will ruin everything.'

'You mustn't,' said Charles anxiously. 'You must be absolutely serious and, if possible, a little intense. We can't hurt the old girl's feelings, however funny she is. You know she is deadly serious about her business.'

Ruth sat on the sofa with her drink. 'I've never quite understood exactly why you need to study Madame Arcati closely,' she said. 'She's absolutely vital to the new novel, is she?'

'Well, yes,' Charles admitted, as he came to join Ruth on the sofa. 'I'm afraid she is.'

'I know you don't like talking about your books while you're still at work on them,' Ruth told him. 'It's a kind of superstition of yours. But you've told me that one of the principal characters is a medium. You understand in general what a medium does, so why is it that you need Madame Arcati?'

Charles thought for a moment, and then said, 'Let me try to explain. Since it's a murder mystery, the plot is extremely complex, but an important part of it – actually not connected with the murder, which takes place later – concerns the theft of a famous painting from a millionaire's home. The millionaire is an art collector, and he has a really fabulous collection. What sets off a chain of events which in due course leads to murder is his apparently chance meeting with another connoisseur. The millionaire's name is Kenneth Fredericks, and the connoisseur whom he meets over drinks at the house of a friend is a Spaniard, Juan di Botello.'

Charles broke off. 'Do you really want to hear all this?' he asked Ruth.

'Certainly, I do,' she replied. 'It already sounds highly intriguing. So Fredericks meets what's-his-name – Botello. What then?'

'I won't go into all the detail,' said Charles, 'but what

happens is that Fredericks invites Botello to come and see his wonderful collection of paintings. Botello comes to the house duly impressed, especially by one painting – a Whistler. Whistler was apparently one of Botello's favourite artists. Fredericks draws his guest's attention to another painting – a famous Rubens, a 'Madonna and Child'. It was the glory of Fredericks' collection, and had cost him – I don't know – several hundred thousand pounds. But Botello, although he appreciates the beauty and the value of the Rubens painting, is clearly more interested in the Whistler watercolour of the Thames. Anyway, while they're looking at the paintings, Botello tells Fredericks that, in addition to being a great lover of classical painting, he is also quite a good painter himself, and he wonders if Fredericks would give him permission to make a copy of the Whistler.'

'Yes? And what then?' Ruth asked.

'Again, I won't divulge the entire plot,' said Charles, 'but I can tell you that Botello is allowed to sit in a room in Fredericks' house and copy the Whistler. Some days later, after he has stopped coming to the house every day to paint his copy of the Whistler, the Rubens goes missing. Botello couldn't have taken it, as he was under surveillance all the time. Well, in due course they find the Rubens, but only to later discover that it's not the original, only a very good copy. It all gets very complicated, and a friend of Fredericks tells him that a certain medium whom he knows – a

German woman called Frau Dosselmann – will be able to trace and find the missing Rubens.'

'And is the Rubens painting found by the medium?' Ruth wanted to know.

'Eventually, yes. But only after all sorts of things have happened,' Charles told her. 'And that's where Madame Arcati will come in handy. For one thing, I need to learn all the jargon.'

Ruth shook her head in wonderment. 'I can understand now why you needed Madame Arcati this evening,' she exclaimed. 'But I wish I hadn't advised you to invite the Bradmans. I'm sure Dr Bradman is as sceptical as we are about that sort of thing – you know, spiritualism and all that. He'll probably say the most dreadful things. Madame Arcati will really have her work cut out.'

'No, no, I've warned him,' Charles assured his wife. 'There have to be more than three people, and we couldn't have had the vicar and his wife because (a) they're dreary, and (b) they probably wouldn't have approved at all, on religious grounds. So it had to be the Bradmans. They'll be fine.'

He was about to continue when Edith rushed into the room with his cigarette case.

'I'm sorry it took so long, sir,' she gasped breathlessly. 'It wasn't where you said it would be, and I had to –'

'It's all right, Edith,' Charles interrupted her. 'Thank

you.' He took the case from her, adding, 'But steady does it, you know. No more galloping.'

'Yes, sir. I mean, no, sir,' Edith responded, still somewhat out of breath. Then, with an obvious effort, she turned and walked slowly out of the room.

Charles watched her go, and then turned to Ruth. 'Perhaps we could make her walk about with a book on her head, like they do in deportment lessons,' he suggested. He walked over to his wife and gave her the cocktail he had mixed for her. 'Here, try this,' he said. 'See if it's to your taste.'

Ruth sipped it. 'Mm. It's lovely. Dry as a bone.'

Charles raised his own glass to her. 'Let's drink a toast to *The Unseen.*'

'I must say that's a wonderful title you've decided on,' Ruth exclaimed.

Charles took a sip of his drink. 'Well, if this evening's a success, I shall be able to get to work seriously on the second chapter tomorrow.'

Ruth smiled up at him. 'How extraordinary it is,' she observed.

'What is?' asked Charles.

'Oh, I don't know. Being in, right at the beginning of something – it gives one an odd feeling.'

Charles nodded in agreement. 'Do you remember,' he asked her, 'how I got the idea for *The Light Goes Out?*'

'Of course I remember,' Ruth assured him, smiling. 'It was when we were on holiday in Biarritz, and we saw that haggard, raddled old woman sitting in the hotel bar. I remember it so well. We sat up half the night talking about her, with you inventing all kinds of stuff. You decided she'd escaped from a nearby lunatic asylum, and we had a number of ideas as to what had driven her mad in the first place. I decided it was an excess of sexual intercourse, but you thought it was more likely an excess of virginity, given her looks.'

'Yes, she certainly came in very handy,' said Charles laughing. 'I often wonder who she was.'

'Who she was or, for that matter, whether she ever knew,' Ruth added. 'I mean, I wonder if she, or anyone who knew her, ever recognised that description of her in your novel – poor thing.' Ruth raised her glass. 'Here's to her, anyhow, and to all such muses,' she exclaimed cheerfully.

She finished her drink, and was about to put her glass down when Charles suggested, 'Have another one, darling.'

'Charles, dear, they're most awfully strong,' she warned him.

'Never mind,' said Charles nonchalantly, as he took Ruth's glass from her.

Ruth watched him as he poured out cocktails for both of them. 'Was Elvira a help to you ever?' she asked. 'When you were thinking something out for one of your novels, I mean,' she added. 'Did she ever come up with ideas for plots, that sort of thing?'

Charles thought for a moment before speaking. Then, 'Occasionally she was helpful – every now and then,' he replied. 'When she concentrated, that is.' He shook his head sadly. 'But she didn't concentrate very often.'

Ruth seemed lost in thought. Then she murmured, 'I do wish I'd known her.'

Charles gave his wife an affectionate look. 'I wonder if you'd have liked her,' he said.

'I'm sure I would,' Ruth replied quickly. 'The way you've always talked about Elvira, she sounds as though she must have been enchanting.' After a few moments' thought, Ruth continued, 'Yes, I'm sure I would have liked her because, you know, I have never for an instant felt in the least bit jealous of her.' She looked at Charles, smiling. 'That's a good sign, isn't it?'

'Yes, I suppose it is,' Charles replied, adding 'Poor Elvira' as he gave Ruth her cocktail.

Ruth looked up at him. 'Does it still hurt – when you think of her?' she asked.

'No, not really,' Charles replied. 'Sometimes I almost wish it did. I don't think of her very often now, but I occasionally remember this or that. But no, it doesn't hurt. I feel rather guilty about that.'

Ruth gazed thoughtfully at him. 'I wonder –' she

murmured. 'I wonder – if I were to die before you'd grown tired of me, I wonder if you'd forget me so soon – and so easily.'

Charles looked shocked. 'Ruth! What a horrible thing to say –'

'No,' Ruth protested. 'I think it's interesting. I'm just not sure how long it would take you to shrug your shoulders and say "Well, that's the end of Ruth. I must start looking for someone else." I can just imagine you saying it.'

She paused and looked seriously at Charles. 'Would it take you long to forget me?' she asked him.

'Well, to begin with,' Charles told her, 'I haven't forgotten Elvira at all. I remember her very distinctly indeed. I remember how fascinating she was, and how maddening as well.' He smiled and continued, 'I remember how badly she played all games and how cross she got when she didn't win.' After a pause, he went on, 'I remember her charm and gaiety when she had achieved her own way over something, and her extreme acidity when she didn't. I remember her physical attractiveness, which was tremendous, and her spiritual integrity, which was nil –'

'You can't remember something that was nil,' Ruth interrupted.

'Well then, I remember her lack of spiritual integrity,' Charles conceded. He attempted to continue his line of thought. 'I certainly remember how morally untidy she was,' he began, only to be interrupted again by Ruth, who asked, 'Was she more physically attractive than I am? Did she have a better figure, a nicer complexion? Did she dress better?'

With a shake of the head, Charles replied suavely, 'Those are very tiresome questions, dear. They fully deserve the wrong answer.'

Ruth smiled at him. 'You really are very sweet,' she admitted.

Charles acknowledged the compliment with a graceful bow. 'Thank you, darling,' he replied.

'But you're a little naive, too,' Ruth continued.

Charles raised his eyebrows. 'Naive? Why?' he asked.

'Because you imagine that I mind about Elvira being more physically attractive than I am,' she replied.

Charles assumed an expression of surprise. 'I should have thought any woman would mind,' he said, adding swiftly, 'If it were true, of course.' Without giving Ruth time to comment, he continued, 'Or perhaps I'm simply old-fashioned in my view of female psychology –'

'Not exactly old-fashioned, darling,' Ruth informed him. 'Just a bit didactic.'

Charles looked curiously at her. 'How do you mean?' he asked.

'Well, what I mean is that it's didactic to attribute to one type the defects of another type,' Ruth explained. 'For instance, just because you know perfectly well that Elvira would have minded terribly if you found another woman more attractive physically than she was, it doesn't necessarily follow that I would mind.'

Ruth paused before adding, emphatically, 'Elvira was a more physical person than I am. I'm quite certain of that – it's all a question of degree.'

Charles gave her a fond smile. 'I love you, my love,' he told her.

'Yes, I know you do, darling,' Ruth replied, 'but you must admit that not the wildest stretch of imagination could describe it as the first fine careless rapture.'

Charles considered this for a moment. 'Would you like it to be?' he enquired, cautiously.

'Good God, no!' was Ruth's instant reply.

Charles laughed. 'Wasn't that just a shade too vehement a response?' he suggested.

Ruth shook her head. 'We're neither of us adolescents, Charles,' she pointed out. 'We've neither of us led exactly prim lives, have we? And we've both been married before. Careless rapture at this stage would be both incongruous and embarrassing.'

'Oh dear, I hope I haven't been in any way a disappointment, my love,' said Charles, trying not to sound too smug.

'Don't be so idiotic,' Ruth told him. 'You know you haven't been in any way disappointing.'

'After all,' Charles continued, 'I believe that your first husband was a great deal older than you, wasn't he? I shouldn't like to think that you'd missed out all along the line. He was generally considered a bit of a bore, wasn't he? And didn't he drink himself to death?'

Ruth looked distinctly annoyed. 'There are moments, Charles,' she snapped, 'when you go too far.'

Charles immediately attempted a contrite expression. 'Sorry, darling,' he replied.

'As far as waspish female psychology goes,' Ruth told him, 'there's a very strong vein of it in *you*.'

'I've heard that said about Julius Caesar, so I'm in very good company,' was Charles's light-hearted response to this.

'Julius Caesar is neither here nor there,' said Ruth impatiently.

'He may be, for all we know,' Charles suggested, flippantly. 'We'll have to ask Madame Arcati. Perhaps she can summon him up for us this evening.'

Ruth clenched her fists in the air. 'You're awfully irritating when you're determined to be witty at all costs,' she exclaimed. She sounded indeed irritable. 'In fact, you're almost supercilious.'

'That's exactly what Elvira used to say,' replied Charles with a smirk of self-satisfaction. 'In the same tone, if not exactly the same words.'

'I'm not at all surprised,' said Ruth. 'I never imagined – physically triumphant and astonishingly attractive as she was – that she was entirely lacking in perception.'

'Darling Ruth!' was Charles's sarcastic response to this.

Ruth raised her hands in a gesture of frustration. 'There you go again,' she exclaimed.

Charles kissed her lightly. 'As I think I may have mentioned before,' he assured her, 'I love you, my love.'

'Poor Elvira,' Ruth muttered.

Charles looked hurt. 'Didn't that gentle, comradely kiss mollify you at all?' he asked her.

'You're very annoying. You know you are,' Ruth told him. 'When I said "Poor Elvira", I assure you it came from the heart. What a terrible life she had with you. You must have bewildered her so horribly.'

'Don't I ever bewilder you at all?' Charles enquired, flippantly.

'Never. Not for an instant,' Ruth answered. 'I know every trick of yours. There's no way you could ever bewilder me.'

Charles laughed. 'Well, all I can say is, in that case we'd better get a divorce immediately,' he suggested. 'Love without a certain degree of bewilderment is pointless, surely.'

Ruth handed him her cocktail glass. 'Put my glass down, there's a darling,' she requested with a fond smile. 'I've had quite enough to drink, and heaven knows what state I'll be in to welcome our guests.'

As he took the glass, Charles continued to think about his first wife. 'You know, Elvira certainly had a great talent for living,' he recalled. 'It was a great pity she died so young.'

Ruth nodded. 'Poor Elvira,' she repeated.

'That remark is becoming a trifle monotonous,' Charles complained. 'Almost a kind of mantra.'

Ruth moved away from him. 'What about "Poor Charles", then,' she suggested.

'Yes, that's better. It's high time I had a little sympathy,' he agreed.

'And later on, "Poor Ruth", I expect,' she continued, in a tone of mock dejection.

Charles shook his head ruefully. 'You have no faith, Ruth,' he told her. 'I really do think you should try to have at least a little faith. Faith in me. Faith in our relationship.'

'I shall strain every nerve,' Ruth promised, sounding not in the least as though she meant it.

Charles wagged a finger at her. 'Life without faith is an arid business,' he advised. 'It's hardly worth living without faith.'

'How beautifully you put things, dear,' Ruth exclaimed.

Charles looked smug. 'I aim to please,' he replied.

Ruth considered him thoughtfully. 'If I died, I wonder

how long it would be before you married again. How long would it take you to find another woman? Can you tell me that?' she asked.

'You won't die,' Charles replied with a derisive snort. 'You're simply not the dying kind.'

'Well, neither was Elvira, surely,' Ruth pointed out.

'Oh yes, she was, now that I look back on it,' said Charles. 'She had a certain ethereal, "not quite of this world" quality, if you know what I mean.' He looked at Ruth, smiling. 'Now, my dear,' he continued, 'nobody could call you even remotely ethereal.'

Ruth pondered whether this was meant as a compliment or an insult. Then, 'Nonsense,' she insisted. 'From all that I've heard about her, Elvira was "of the earth", earthy.'

'Well, she is now, anyhow,' Charles observed with a heartlessly dismissive chuckle.

Ruth shook her head angrily. 'You know, Charles, that's the kind of observation that shocks people,' she warned him. 'You sometimes go too far.'

'Yes, I suppose I do,' Charles admitted. 'But I don't mind shocking people. It's discouraging to think how many people are shocked by honesty, and how few by deceit.'

'You'd better write that down,' Ruth advised him sarcastically. 'Otherwise, you might forget it.'

'Darling, you underestimate me,' Charles replied smugly.

'Anyway, you weren't being honest,' Ruth continued.

24

'You were just indulging in your customary bad taste. Can't you ever give it a rest?'

Charles was silent for a moment or two before replying. Then he said, 'Let's be serious about this, for a change. I was devoted to Elvira. We were married for five years. She died. I missed her very much. That was seven years ago. I have now – with your help, my love – risen above the whole thing. *Oublions le passé*, as some French writer said somewhere.'

'So you've risen above the whole thing. Admirable,' Ruth congratulated him. 'But if tragedy should ever darken our lives, I still say – with prophetic foreboding – poor me!'

While she was speaking, a bell rang, and continued to ring. 'That's probably the Bradmans arriving,' said Charles.

'How do you know? Are you psychic? It might be Madame Arcati,' Ruth suggested.

'Yes,' he agreed. 'It could well be. She'll have to come on her bicycle, of course. She always goes everywhere on her bicycle. She criss-crosses the village in a manner that people say presents a hazard to motorists and pedestrians alike.'

Ruth smiled. 'It really is very spirited of the old girl.'

'Shall I go and answer the door?' Charles wondered. 'Or shall we let Edith have her fling?'

'Let's wait a minute and see what happens,' Ruth advised.

There was a slight pause. When the doorbell rang again,

Charles observed, 'Perhaps Edith didn't hear, if she's in the kitchen.'

'She's probably on one knee in pre-sprinting position, waiting for cook to open the kitchen door,' suggested Ruth, laughing.

There was the sound of a door banging inside the house. Looking out into the hall, Charles saw Edith scampering across to the front door. 'Steady, Edith,' he called out to her.

'Yes, sir,' the maid answered, dropping to a walk. Charles and Ruth smiled at each other as they heard her opening the front door.

Chapter Three

———

A few moments later, Edith ushered two people into the room. 'Doctor and Mrs Bradman,' she announced in a sober and deliberate tone. She took the guests' coats and left to go back to the kitchen, while Charles went over to greet the visitors as they entered. Dr Bradman was a pleasant-looking, middle-aged man of medium height, his hair and moustache flecked with grey, and his wife was a fair-haired, well-preserved lady of roughly the same age.

Mrs Bradman crossed the room to shake hands with Ruth, and Charles Condomine shook hands with the doctor.

'We're not late, are we?' Dr Bradman asked. 'I'm afraid I only got back from the hospital about half an hour ago. We had a terrible day with the flu outbreak.'

'No, you're not at all late,' Charles assured him. 'Madame

Arcati isn't here yet, but I'm sure she'll be with us quite soon.'

'Oh, that must have been her we passed coming down the hill,' Mrs Bradman exclaimed. 'It was hard to see in the dark, but I said I thought it was.'

'Then she won't be long. Anyway, I'm glad you were able to come,' said Ruth, flashing a welcoming smile at the Bradmans.

'We've been looking forward to this so much,' Mrs Bradman told her. 'I really feel quite excited at the thought of participating in a seance.'

'Well, don't get overexcited, Violet,' Dr Bradman admonished his wife with a laugh. Turning to his hosts, he continued lightheartedly, 'I guarantee that Violet will behave herself. I made her promise.'

'There wasn't any need — I'm always far too well behaved,' Mrs Bradman assured the Condomines, sharing in her husband's laughter. 'But it's true that I'm absolutely thrilled at the thought of this evening. I've encountered Madame Arcati two or three times in the village, but I've never seen her in action, so to speak. I've never seen her do anything at all peculiar, if you know what I mean.' Her face was flushed with obvious anticipation of a thrilling new experience.

Charles Condomine had gone over to the cocktail table. 'Dry Martinis?' he asked Dr Bradman, who replied, 'By all means. We're both fond of our Martinis.' With a light-hearted gesture at his wife, he continued, 'In fact, Violet is a little too fond of them. I could tell you about one occasion when –'

Violet Bradman interrupted him. 'Don't you dare, Stephen!' she warned him, with a laugh.

'Which reminds me that I'll have another Martini, Charles,' said Ruth. 'But not quite so strong this time, please.'

'Madame Arcati certainly is a strange woman,' Charles told the Bradmans, as he mixed their drinks. 'It was only a chance remark of the vicar's about seeing her up on the knoll on Midsummer Eve dressed in sort of Indian robes that made me realise that she was psychic at all, or interested in that kind of thing. Then I began to make enquiries. Apparently she's been a professional medium in London for years. She had a large following there, but eventually she felt it was time to take it a little more easily, down here in the country.'

Mrs Bradman shook her head, looking perplexed. 'It is funny, isn't it?' she observed. 'I mean, anybody doing it as a profession.'

'Not all that funny,' her husband countered. 'I believe it's a very lucrative profession, presiding over seances, conjuring up spirits, and all that kind of thing.'

Violet Bradman turned to Ruth. 'Do you believe in it,

Mrs Condomine?' she enquired. 'Do you think there's anything really genuine about it all?'

Ruth gave a regretful smile. 'I'm afraid not,' she answered. 'I'm a complete sceptic. But I do think it's interesting how easily people can allow themselves to be deceived.'

'But she must believe it herself, mustn't she?' Mrs Bradman asked. 'Or is the whole business a fake?' There was a touch of indignation in her voice at the thought of such possible trickery.

Charles Condomine put the final touch to the Martinis he had been mixing at the cocktail table, and turned with drinks in his hands. 'Well, I suspect the worst,' he told the Bradmans. 'A real professional charlatan is what I think she'll turn out to be. That's what I'm hoping for, anyhow. You see, the character I'm planning for my book has to be a complete imposter. That's one of the most important factors of the whole story, and I simply must get it right.'

'What exactly are you hoping to get from Madame Arcati this evening?' Dr Bradman asked him.

'Jargon, principally,' Charles replied as he handed their drinks to the doctor and his wife. 'A few tricks of the trade, perhaps. After all, I haven't been to a seance for years, and I want to refresh my memory.'

'Then it's not entirely new to you?' Dr Bradman asked with surprise, downing his drink in one gulp.

'Oh no,' replied Charles. 'It's not entirely new.' Smiling, he continued, 'When I was a little boy, an aunt of mine used to come and stay with us. She imagined that she was a medium, and she used to go off into the most elaborate trances after dinner. My mother was fascinated by it, as was the whole family.'

'But was your mother convinced by it?' Mrs Bradman wanted to know.

Charles gave a laugh. 'Good heavens, no,' he replied. She just naturally disliked my aunt and loved making a fool of her.' He went across to the cocktail table to mix another drink for himself and for Dr Bradman.

Dr Bradman smiled. 'I gather that there were never any tangible results?' he surmised. 'No real proof of her powers?'

'Oh, sometimes she didn't do so badly,' Charles replied. 'On one occasion, when we were all sitting around in the pitch dark with my mother at the piano groping her way through a little piece by Chaminade, my aunt suddenly gave a shrill scream and said that she could see a small black dog close to my chair. Then someone switched on the lights, and sure enough there it was.'

Mrs Bradman gasped. 'But how extraordinary! You must all have been amazed.'

'Well, not really,' Charles admitted. 'It was obviously a stray that had come in from the street in search of a meal.

But I must say I took off my hat to Auntie for producing it, or rather utilising it. Even mother was a bit shaken.' He chuckled at the recollection of it.

'What happened to the poor little dog?' Mrs Bradman wanted to know.

Charles laughed. 'Oh, it lived with us for years, without any further brushes with the paranormal,' he told her. 'It was a male dog. We gave it a name – Rudi.'

Ruth Condomine looked slightly apprehensive. 'I sincerely hope Madame Arcati won't produce any livestock this evening,' she exclaimed. 'As you can see, we have so very little room in this house.'

'Do you think she tells fortunes?' Mrs Bradman wondered. 'I love having my fortune told.'

'I expect she does, because –' Charles began, but he was interrupted by Ruth, who announced, 'I was told once, on the pier at Southsea, that I was surrounded by lilies and a golden seven. It worried me for days, trying to puzzle out what it meant. I never did, of course.'

The others all laughed. Then Charles assumed a grave expression. 'We really must all be serious, you know,' he admonished them. 'We must pretend that we believe implicitly. Otherwise, she won't play.'

'Also,' Ruth pointed out, 'she might really mind. And it would be cruel to upset her.'

'I shall be as good as gold,' Dr Bradman promised.

'Have you ever attended her, Doctor? Professionally, I mean?' Ruth asked him.

'Yes,' Dr Bradman replied. 'She had influenza in January – she's only been here just over a year, you know.' He paused, trying to remember, and then continued, 'I must say she was singularly un-psychic then.'

He turned to Charles. 'I always understood that she was an author – or does one say authoress?' he asked.

'I'm never sure whether the feminists like to be referred to as authors or authoresses. But, oh, yes,' Charles told him, 'we originally met as colleagues at one of those Sunday literary evenings run by that woman in Sandgate, where anybody who can string two words together turns up as a self-declared author. I used to go along and lecture to them occasionally, but I've stopped doing it now – it was too boring.'

'What sort of books does Madame Arcati write?' Mrs Bradman wanted to know.

'Two kinds,' said Charles. 'Rather whimsical children's stories about enchanted woods filled with highly conversational flora and fauna, and enthusiastic biographies of minor members of the royal family, very sentimental, reverent, and extremely funny – unintentionally, of course.'

They all laughed, then stopped when they heard the sound of the front-door bell. 'Here she is,' Ruth announced.

'She knows, doesn't she, about tonight?' Dr Bradman asked. 'About the seance, I mean. You're not going to spring it on her suddenly?'

'No, she certainly knows,' Charles assured him. 'It was all arranged last week. I told her how profoundly interested I was in anything to do with the occult, and she blossomed like a rose. When I suggested we might have a seance, she leapt at the idea immediately. I didn't have to do any persuading.'

Ruth gave a slight shiver. 'I really feel quite nervous,' she confessed. 'As though I were going to make a speech and I hadn't properly prepared it.'

Edith entered the room from the hall, and everyone watched her as she made her way sedately towards the front door.

'Why don't you go and meet Madame Arcati, darling?' Charles suggested to his wife. Meanwhile, Edith had opened the door, and the medium's voice, very high and clear, could be heard. 'I've leaned my bike up against that little bush outside,' she was telling the maid. 'I'm sure it will be perfectly all right there if nobody touches it.'

Edith came in to announce, 'Madame Arcati,' and that lady entered the room, pausing at the door to hand a rather beaten-up raincoat to the maid.

Madame Arcati was a striking woman, dressed not too extravagantly but with a decided bias towards the barbaric.

Her jewellery consisted of chains and bangles which rattled as she made her way into the room to be greeted by the assembled company. She looked as though she could be any age between forty-five and sixty.

'How nice of you to have come all this way,' Ruth welcomed her, ushering her into the room, while Charles advanced to greet her with 'My dear Madame Arcati.'

'I'm afraid I'm rather late,' Madame Arcati apologised, 'but I had a sudden presentiment that I was going to have a puncture, so I went back to fetch my pump.'

She looked around at everyone before continuing, 'And then, of course, I didn't have a puncture at all.'

'Never mind,' Charles consoled her. 'You can't be too careful. Perhaps you'll have a puncture on your way home.'

Madame Arcati nodded gravely and went across to shake hands with the doctor. 'Dr Bradman,' she greeted him sweetly. 'The man with such gentle hands!'

'I'm delighted to see you looking so well,' Dr Bradman told her. He gestured towards Mrs Bradman. 'This is my wife.'

'We are old friends,' Madame Arcati told him as, still wearing her gloves, she shook hands with Mrs Bradman over the back of the sofa. 'We meet coming out of shops. Very nice to meet you properly, as it were, Mrs Bradman.'

Charles Condomine gave the medium a welcoming smile. 'Would you like a cocktail?' he asked her.

Peeling off her rather strange-looking gloves to reveal a collection of exotic rings, Madame Arcati replied, 'If it's a dry Martini, yes. If it's any other concoction, no.' She shuddered comically. 'Experience has taught me to be very wary of concoctions.'

'It is a dry Martini,' Charles assured her.

'How delicious!' Madame Arcati exclaimed, smacking her lips in anticipation. She looked about her, taking them all in with her glance. 'It was wonderful cycling through the woods this evening,' she told them. 'I was deafened with birdsong.'

'It's been lovely all day,' Ruth agreed.

'Ah, but the evening's the time,' Madame Arcati insisted. 'Mark my words.' She accepted the cocktail Charles handed to her. 'Thank you. Cheers!' she toasted, raising her glass to the company. 'Cheers!'

They sipped their drinks. There was a pause. Then, 'Don't you find it very tiring, bicycling everywhere?' Ruth asked Madame Arcati, who replied, 'On the contrary, it stimulates me. I was getting far too sedentary in London, in my horrid little flat with the dim lights.' Addressing Charles, she explained, 'The lights have to be dim, you know. The clients expect it.'

There was a moment's silence, broken by Mrs Bradman with the comment, 'I must say I find bicycling very exhausting.'

Madame Arcati gave her a somewhat pitying look. 'Steady rhythm,' she advised, 'that's what counts.'

When Mrs Bradman looked dubious at this, Madame Arcati continued, 'Once you get the knack of it, you need never look back.' She waved her arms enthusiastically. 'On you get, and away you go.'

'But what about the hills, Madame Arcati?' the doctor's wife persisted. 'There are so many hills around here. It must be awfully difficult, pushing up those awful hills –'

'It's just the knack of it again,' the medium told her, before tossing down her Martini. She added, 'Down with your head, up with your heart, and you're over the top in a flash, and skimming down the other side like a dragonfly.'

Mrs Bradman looked unconvinced by this unlikely image, and was about to speak again when Madame Arcati announced to their host, 'That was the best dry Martini I've had for years.'

Charles beamed at her. 'Will you have another?' he asked.

'Certainly,' Madame Arcati replied immediately, holding out her glass. As Charles took it from her, she went on, 'You know, you're a very clever man, Mr Condomine. Anybody can write books, but it takes a real artist to make a dry Martini that's dry enough.'

Charles accepted the compliment with a little bow, and Ruth asked, ' Are *you* writing anything nowadays, Madame Arcati?'

Nodding briskly, Madame Arcati replied, 'Indeed I am. Every morning, as regular as clockwork. From seven till one.'

Handing her another Martini, Charles asked, 'Is it a novel or a memoir that you're working on at present?'

'Neither, my dear Mr Condomine. It's a children's book,' she told him. 'I have to finish it by the end of September to catch the Christmas sales. It's mostly about very small animals, and the hero is a moss beetle.'

Mrs Bradman laughed nervously at this further reference to an insect, and was rewarded with a stern glance from Madame Arcati, who continued, 'I had to give up my memoir of Princess Palliatani because she died unexpectedly in Monte Carlo in April. I talked to her about it the other day, and she implored me to go on with it, but I really hadn't the heart.'

'You *talked* to her about it the other day?' Mrs Bradman asked, again with a nervous laugh.

'Yes,' the medium replied. 'Through my control, of course. She sounded very irritable – not at all like her, really.'

Trying to look serious, Mrs Bradman commented, 'It's odd to think of people in the spirit world being irritable, isn't it? I mean, one can hardly imagine it, can one? I know I can't grasp the idea.'

'Well, after all,' said Charles, 'we have no reliable

guarantee that the afterlife will be any less exasperating than this one, have we?'

'Oh, Mr Condomine, how *can* you?' Mrs Bradman gasped, trying not to laugh.

Addressing Madame Arcati, Ruth asked, 'I expect it's dreadfully ignorant of me not to know – but who was Princess Palliatani?'

'She was originally a Jewess from Odessa of quite remarkable beauty,' replied the medium gravely. 'It was a very well-known fact that people used to stand on the seats of railway stations to watch her whizz by in the train.'

'She was a keen traveller?' Charles asked.

'In her younger days, yes,' he was told. 'Later on, she married a Mr Clarke in the Consular Service, and settled down for a while –'

Madame Arcati paused, seemingly lost in recollection, and Ruth took the opportunity to ask, 'But how did she become Princess Palliatani?'

'That was years later,' Madame Arcati replied. 'Mr Clarke passed over, and left her penniless with two strapping girls –'

'How unpleasant!' Ruth exclaimed, as Madame Arcati continued, 'And so there was nothing for it but to obey the beckoning finger of adventure and take to the road again.' She waved her arms in the air. 'So off she went, bag and baggage, to Vladivostock.'

'What an extraordinary place to go to,' Charles exclaimed.

'That long and ghastly train journey through Russia to the end of the world, with people standing on the seats at every little station to catch a glimpse of you.'

Madame Arcati wagged a finger in his face. 'She had cousins there,' she exclaimed triumphantly. 'And some years later she met old Palliatani who was returning from a highly secret mission in Japan or somewhere like that. He was immediately staggered by her beauty, and very shortly afterwards he married her.' She paused and then continued, meaningfully, 'From then on her life became really interesting.'

'I should hardly have described it as dull before,' murmured Dr Bradman, while Ruth asked, 'What happened to the two children – the two strapping girls?'

Madame Arcati was silent for a moment or two, for what she clearly intended as dramatic effect. Then she announced, 'She neither saw them nor spoke to them for twenty-three years.'

'How extraordinary!' Mrs Bradman exclaimed, but Madame Arcati immediately corrected her. 'Not at all,' the medium said. 'She was always very erratic emotionally.'

Suddenly, the double doors of the dining room opened, and Edith came in, announcing nervously to Ruth, 'Dinner is served, ma'am.'

'Thank you, Edith,' said Ruth, and then, addressing her guests, added, with a gesture, 'Shall we – ?'

Edith retired backwards to the dining room. As they prepared to follow her, Madame Arcati asked, 'No red meat, I hope?'

'There's meat,' Ruth told her, 'but I don't think it will be very red. Would you rather have a purely vegetarian dish – an egg or something?'

'No, thank you,' the medium replied. 'It's just that I make it a rule never to eat red meat before I start working – it sometimes has a very odd effect –'

'What sort of effect?' asked Charles, curiously.

'Oh, nothing of the least importance,' Madame Arcati assured him. 'If it isn't very red, it won't matter much. Anyhow, we'll risk it.'

She went out first, with Ruth, followed by Mrs Bradman, Dr Bradman and Charles.

'Come along, then,' Ruth called to the others as they moved into the dining room. She indicated the various places at the table. 'Mrs Bradman, you're there. Madame Arcati, you're on my husband's right . . .'

They all took their places around the dining table, and sat.

Chapter Four

——▪——

An hour or so later, at the end of a splendid meal, Ruth Condomine rose and addressed the other two women at the table. 'Shall we leave the gentlemen to their cigars and cognac or whatever, and have our coffee in the living room?' she suggested.

Mrs Bradman and Madame Arcati nodded their agreement, and the women went back into the living room. Edith was already standing by the coffee table, and poured coffee for Mrs Bradman, who seated herself on a pouffe, and for Madame Arcati who made herself comfortable on the sofa, and for Ruth who sat next to the medium. Madame Arcati had already begun to tell the doctor's wife about a recent successful seance.

'Yes, on her mother's side she went right back to the

Borgias,' Madame Arcati was explaining enthusiastically. 'I think that accounted for a lot, one way or the other. Even as a child, you know, she was given to the most violent destructive tempers.' She gave a fierce shake of the head. 'Very inbred, very, very inbred,' she exclaimed.

'Yes, she must have been,' Mrs Bradman responded, not quite sure whether she had followed Madame Arcati's narrative clearly.

The medium continued with her story. 'Actually, my control was quite scared the other day, when we were talking,' she told Mrs Bradman. 'I could hear it in her voice. After all, she's only a child.'

Mrs Bradman and Ruth both looked puzzled. 'Do you always have a child as a control, or whatever you call it?' Ruth asked.

'Yes, they're generally the best,' Madame Arcati told her, nodding enthusiastically. 'Some mediums prefer Red Indians of course, but personally I've always found them most unreliable.'

Not surprisingly, Ruth failed to understand this. 'In what way unreliable?' she wanted to know.

Madame Arcati settled herself more comfortably into the sofa. 'Well,' she replied, 'for one thing they're frightfully lazy. And also, when they're faced with any sort of difficulty, they're rather apt to go off into their own tribal language which is naturally unintelligible.' She shrugged her shoulders. 'That generally spoils everything and wastes a great deal of time.'

'Yes, I suppose it does,' Ruth murmured.

The medium sat up, looked around at her two listeners and, wagging a finger for emphasis, continued, 'No. Children are undoubtedly more satisfactory.' After a moment's thought, she added, 'Particularly when they get to know you and understand your ways.' She gave a sigh of contentment. 'Daphne,' she informed them, 'has worked with me for many years.'

Mrs Bradman looked perplexed. 'But she still – Daphne, I mean – she still goes on being a child?' she asked. 'I mean, she doesn't show signs of growing any older?'

Madame Arcati regarded her with an air of superiority. 'Time values on the other side,' she explained patiently, articulating the words 'other side' as though they were in capital letters, 'are utterly different from ours.'

Gazing at her in wonderment, Mrs Bradman asked, 'Tell me, do you feel funny when you go off in a trance?'

'In what way funny?' Madame Arcati responded, looking and sounding more than a trifle offended.

Ruth intervened hastily. 'I'm sure Mrs Bradman doesn't mean funny in its comic implication,' she began. 'I think she meant odd or strange –'

Madame Arcati interrupted her. 'The word was an unfortunate choice,' she said, sounding quite terse.

'I'm sure I'm very sorry,' Mrs Bradman told her hastily.

'It doesn't matter in the least,' replied the medium with lofty dignity. 'Please don't apologise.'

After an awkward pause, Ruth attempted to put the conversation back on an even keel again. 'When did you discover that you had these extraordinary powers?' she asked Madame Arcati.

'When I was quite tiny,' Madame Arcati replied. 'My mother was a medium before me, you know, and so I had every opportunity of starting on the ground floor, as you might say.'

After a pause for effect, the medium continued, 'I had my first trance when I was four years old, and my first ectoplasmic manifestation when I was five and a half.' She thought for a moment, obviously remembering the occasion fondly. 'What an exciting day that was. I shall never forget it.'

Rapt in wonderment, her hearers were silent. 'Of course,' Madame Arcati informed them, 'the manifestation was quite small and of very short duration, but for a child of my tender years it was most gratifying.'

Mrs Bradman made an attempt to ingratiate herself with the medium. 'Your mother must have been so pleased,' she exclaimed.

'She was,' Madame Arcati agreed, making no attempt to look or sound modest.

'Can you foretell the future?' the doctor's wife asked her, eagerly.

'Certainly not,' Madame Arcati snapped. 'I disapprove of fortune-tellers most strongly.'

Mrs Bradman looked disappointed. 'Oh, really? Why?' she asked.

Madame Arcati waved a hand dismissively. 'There's too much guesswork and fake mixed up with it, even when the gift is genuine,' she explained. 'And it only very occasionally *is* genuine. You can't count on it at all.'

'Why not?' Ruth wondered aloud.

'It's Time again,' the medium replied. 'It always is. Time is the reef –' she continued portentously, 'the reef upon which all our frail mystic ships are wrecked.'

Ruth pondered this. 'I suppose you mean,' she suggested after a pause, 'because it has never yet been proved that the past and the present and the future are not one and the same thing.'

Madame Arcati nodded her head gravely. 'I long ago came to the conclusion,' she announced, 'that nothing has ever been definitely proved about anything.'

'How very wise' was Ruth's somewhat inadequate reply to this.

Madame Arcati gulped down the remnants of her coffee, and handed her cup to Ruth. Mrs Bradman, finishing her coffee simultaneously, put her cup behind her on a small table as Edith came into the room with a tray of drinks. The maid put the tray down on a table near Ruth, who moved a vase and her coffee cup to make room for it. She also removed a cigarette box and an ashtray from the table and gave them to Edith, who put them on the drinks table.

'I want you to leave the dining room just as it is for tonight, Edith,' Ruth told the maid. 'You can clear the table in the morning.'

Not surprisingly, 'Yes'm' was Edith's reply.

'And we don't want to be disturbed in here for the next hour or so, for any reason whatsoever,' Ruth told her. 'Is that clear?'

'Yes'm.' Edith turned to go, but stopped as Ruth continued, 'And if anyone should telephone, just say we are out and take a message.'

'Unless it's an urgent call for Dr Bradman,' the doctor's wife felt obliged to point out.

'Unless, of course, it's an urgent call for Dr Bradman,' Ruth confirmed.

'Yes'm,' Edith replied, and left the room swiftly.

Ruth turned to the doctor's wife. 'There isn't likely to be a call, is there?' she asked.

'No, I don't think it's at all likely,' Mrs Bradman assured her. 'but I thought I ought to spell it out, just in case.'

Madame Arcati looked concerned. 'Once I am off in a

trance, it won't matter,' she explained, 'But an interruption during the preliminary stages might be disastrous.'

This was greeted in uneasy silence. Then, after a pause, Mrs Bradman said, 'Oh, I do wish the men would hurry up. I'm getting terribly excited.'

'Please try not to be,' Madame Arcati warned her with a frown. 'It makes everything much more difficult.'

Mrs Bradman was about to respond, when her husband and Charles Condomine came in from the dining room, both of them smoking cigars.

'Well, Madame Arcati,' Charles exclaimed in gleeful anticipation, 'the time is drawing near.'

'Who knows?' the medium responded suavely. 'It may be receding!'

'How very true,' Charles observed, while Dr Bradman asked, sounding somewhat anxious, 'I hope you feel in the mood, Madame Arcati.'

Madame Arcati glared at the doctor. 'It isn't a question of mood,' she told him, sharply. 'It's a question of concentration.'

Fearing the medium might perhaps be feeling rushed, Ruth said, 'You must forgive us for being so impatient. This is all completely new and exciting for us. We can perfectly easily wait, of course, if you're not quite ready to start –'

'Nonsense, my dear,' Madame Arcati interrupted her,

vigorously. 'I'm absolutely ready.' She rose from the sofa with a cry of 'Heigho, heigho, it's off to work we go!'

Charles gave her a quizzical look. 'Is there anything at all that you'd like us to do?' he asked.

The medium looked perplexed. 'Do?' she repeated.

'Yes,' said Charles. 'You know – like holding hands or anything.'

Madame Arcati shook her head with vigour. 'All that will come later,' she promised. She went to the French windows and opened them, while the others stood up in anticipation of action of some kind or another.

'First and most important of all, I take a few deep breaths of fresh air,' Madame Arcati announced to the company over her shoulder. 'You may talk if you wish – it will not disturb me in the least.' Flinging the windows open more widely, she inhaled deeply and more than a trifle noisily.

'Oh, dear,' Ruth murmured, with a quizzical glance at Charles.

Her husband put a finger to his lips warningly. 'An excellent dinner, Ruth,' he said very loudly. 'I congratulate you. But then your meals are always superb.'

Ruth shook her head. 'The mousse wasn't quite right,' she confessed.

Charles cast a beaming smile around the room. 'It might have looked a bit hysterical,' he recalled, 'but it tasted delicious.'

Ruth was about to speak again, when the voice of Madame Arcati boomed at them from the French windows. 'That cuckoo is very angry,' she declared.

The Condomines and the Bradmans cast puzzled glances at one another. 'I beg your pardon?' Charles asked.

'I said that the cuckoo over there in the tree is very angry,' Madame Arcati explained. 'Just listen to the noise it's making.'

They all listened obediently, and indeed a cuckoo obliged with a cuckoo-like sound. They all looked at one another, puzzled, and Charles asked the medium, 'How can you tell it's angry?'

'Its timbre,' Madame Arcati informed him bluntly and not very helpfully. Then, still looking out of the windows, she continued, 'There's no moon tonight. That's just as well, I think. And there's a mist rising from the marshes.'

A thought suddenly struck her. Turning to face the Condomines, she asked, sounding quite anxious, 'There's no need for me to light my bicycle lamp, is there? I mean, nobody is likely to fall over it?'

'No,' Ruth assured her. 'There's no chance of that. We're not expecting anybody else this evening.'

Madame Arcati gave a nod of satisfaction. She closed the windows, calling to the cuckoo as she did so, 'Goodnight, you foolish bird.' Then, returning to the centre of the room, she looked about her. 'Do you have a table we can use?' she asked her hosts.

'Yes, of course,' Charles replied. He gestured to the small table by the piano. 'We thought perhaps that one would do.'

Madame Arcati put her hands on the table that he had indicated, and then shook her head. Looking about her, she pointed to the drinks table. 'I think that the one over there with the drinks on would be better,' she decided.

'Come on, then. Let's change over,' said Dr Bradman, suiting the action to the word, and removing the tray of drinks to the smaller table.

'You told Edith we didn't want to be disturbed, didn't you?' Charles asked Ruth, who replied, 'Yes, Charles. Of course I did.'

They all turned to observe Madame Arcati who was now walking about the room, wringing her hands. When she saw that they were watching her, she explained, 'This is a moment I always hate.'

'Are you nervous?' Ruth asked her, solicitously.

'Yes,' the medium admitted. 'When I was a girl, I always used to be sick at this point.'

Dr Bradman allowed himself a surreptitious smile. 'How fortunate that you grew out of it,' he observed.

Obviously fearing that Madame Arcati might regard this as an unhelpful remark, Ruth chimed in quickly. 'Children are always much more prone to be sick than grown-ups, aren't they?' she asked the company in general. 'I know I could never travel in a train with any degree of safety until I was fourteen.'

She laughed as she remembered, and Dr Bradman nodded his head in agreement. 'Yes, you're right about children,' he observed.

Madame Arcati, however, was completely oblivious to their comments. Still walking around the room, she was now chanting. 'Little Tommy Tucker sings for his supper. What shall he have but brown bread and butter?' She paused, and then said to the others, 'I despise that little jingle because it doesn't rhyme at all – but Daphne loves it.'

'Who is Daphne?' Dr Bradman asked, looking perplexed.

'Daphne is Madame Arcati's control,' Ruth told him. 'She's a little girl.'

'Oh, I see,' the doctor replied. 'Yes, of course.' However, he still looked perplexed.

'How old is Daphne?' Charles asked.

'She was almost seven when she died,' Madame Arcati told him, brusquely.

'And when was that?' Mrs Bradman wanted to know.

'February the sixth, 1884,' came the medium's prompt reply.

'Poor little thing,' Mrs Bradman murmured, trying to suppress a smile, while her husband added, 'She must be a bit long in the tooth by now, I should think.'

Madame Arcati abruptly ceased her peregrination around the room, and addressed the doctor. 'You *should* think, Dr Bradman,' she snapped, 'but I fear you don't. At least, not profoundly enough.'

'Do be quiet, George,' Mrs Bradman admonished her husband. 'You'll put Madame Arcati off.'

Turning to her, the medium spoke reassuringly. 'Don't worry, my dear,' she said with what she no doubt intended as a gracious smile. 'I am quite used to sceptics. They generally turn out to be the most vulnerable and receptive of believers in the long run.'

'Now, you'd better take that to heart, Dr Bradman,' Ruth warned him jovially.

The doctor hastened to express his remorse. 'Please forgive me, Madame Arcati,' he begged her. 'I assure you I am most deeply interested.'

'It is of no consequence,' the medium replied grandly. Then, addressing them all, she continued, 'Will you all sit around the table, please, and place your hands downwards on it.'

Ruth gestured to the doctor's wife. 'Come, Mrs Bradman,' she invited her, moving towards the table.

'What about the lights?' Charles asked.

'All in good time, Mr Condomine,' Madame Arcati assured him. 'Sit down, please.'

The four of them sat on either side of the small square table, and Madame Arcati surveyed them critically, her head on one side. She was whistling a little tune, but broke off to say, 'The fingers should be touching.'

They did as they were told. 'That's right. Very good,' she encouraged them. Then, gesturing to the other side of the room, she said, 'I presume that is the gramophone, Mr Condomine?'

'Yes,' Charles replied, half rising. 'Would you like me to start it for you?'

'Please stay where you are,' Madame Arcati told him. 'I can manage it by myself.' She went across to the gramophone and looked over a pile of discs lying beside it. 'Now let me see,' she mused. 'What have we here? Brahms – oh, dear me, no . . . Rakhmaninov – too florid.' She turned around to address Charles. 'Where is the dance music, Mr Condomine?' she asked.

Charles looked as though he had no idea, and it was Ruth who answered her. 'They're the ones underneath,' she called across the room.

'I see,' Madame Arcati said as she stooped down and picked up another pile of discs.

'I'm afraid none of them are very new,' Charles warned her.

'Oh, that doesn't matter,' the medium replied. She looked at the discs she was holding. 'Ah, here's a good one,' she exclaimed. 'It's songs by Irving Berlin.' She turned to face the Condomines again. 'Now, Daphne is really more attached to Irving Berlin than to any other composer,' she told them. 'She likes a tune she can hum.' She consulted the list of songs on the disc. 'Ah, let's have the first song – "Always",' she announced.

Charles Condomine half jumped out of his chair with a start. "Always"!' he exclaimed.

'Do sit down, Charles,' his wife admonished him. 'What's the matter with you?'

Charles subsided. 'Oh, nothing – nothing at all,' he replied, unconvincingly.

Madame Arcati approached the table where they were sitting. 'The light switch is by the door, I suppose?' she asked Ruth.

'Yes,' Ruth replied. 'Just to the left of the door. It controls all the lights in the room except the small light on the desk, and of course the gramophone.'

Madame Arcati nodded. 'Very well – I understand.'

'Charles, do keep still,' Ruth murmured to her husband who was fidgeting nervously.

'Our fingers must be touching, George,' Mrs Bradman reminded the doctor. 'Remember what Madame Arcati told us.'

'Now,' said the medium, clapping her hands for attention, 'there are one or two things that I should like to explain, so will you all please listen attentively?'

'Of course,' Ruth assured her.

'Presently, when the music begins, I am going to switch out the lights,' Madame Arcati announced. 'I may then walk about the room for a little, or perhaps lie down flat. In due course I shall draw up this dear little stool' – she waved affectionately at the stool – 'and join you at the table. I shall place myself between you and your wife, Mr Condomine, and rest my hands lightly upon yours.'

She paused, and then added emphatically, 'I must ask you not to address me, or move, or do anything in the least distracting.' She looked at each of them in turn. 'Is that quite, quite clear?' she asked.

'Perfectly,' Charles replied, and the others murmured their agreement.

'Of course,' Madame Arcati continued, 'I cannot guarantee that anything will happen at all. For one thing, Daphne may be unavailable. She had a bad cold very recently, and was rather under the weather, poor child. On the other hand, a great many things might occur.'

She looked earnestly at each of her listeners in turn as she went on. 'One of you might have an emanation, for instance. Or we might contact a poltergeist, which would be extremely destructive and noisy –'

Ruth interrupted her. 'In what way destructive?' she asked anxiously.

'Poltergeists are inclined to throw things, you know,' the medium explained.

Ruth looked apprehensive. 'I didn't know,' she admitted.

'But we must cross that bridge when we come to it, mustn't we?' Madame Arcati asked, again looking at each of them in turn.

'Certainly – by all means,' Charles assured her, though he himself looked more than a trifle apprehensive.

'Fortunately,' the medium continued, 'An Elemental at this time of year is most unlikely.'

Ruth looked even more apprehensive than Charles. 'What do Elementals do?' she wanted to know.

The medium shrugged her shoulders. 'Oh, my dear, one can never tell,' she admitted. 'They're dreadfully unpredictable, you know. Usually, they take the form of a very cold wind –'

'I don't think I shall like that,' Mrs Bradman muttered, shivering at the thought.

Madame Arcati shot her a stern glance, before continuing, 'a very cold wind, occasionally reaching almost hurricane velocity –'

Ruth interrupted her. 'You don't think that perhaps it would be a good idea to take the more breakable ornaments off the mantelpiece before we start?' she asked anxiously.

'That really is not necessary, Mrs Condomine,' Madame

Arcati replied with an indulgent smile. 'I can assure you that I have my own method of dealing with Elementals.'

'I'm so glad,' said Ruth, her expression failing to match her words.

Clapping her hands together again, the medium asked, 'Now then – are you all ready to empty your minds?'

'Do you mean we must try to think of nothing?' Dr Bradman asked her.

Madame Arcati nodded emphatically. 'Absolutely nothing, Dr Bradman,' she confirmed. 'I suggest you concentrate on a space or a nondescript colour – that's really the safest way.'

'I'll do my best,' the doctor promised.

'Good work!' the medium congratulated him. 'I will now start the music,' she announced.

She went to the gramophone, and put on the first track of the disc of Irving Berlin numbers, which was the song 'Always'. She then began to walk about the room, occasionally moving into an abortive little dance step. At one moment, as she passed a mirror on the mantelpiece, she surveyed herself critically for a moment and adjusted her hair. Then, with a sudden burst of speed, she ran across the room and switched off the lights.

'Oh, dear!' Mrs Bradman exclaimed, only to be immediately admonished by Madame Arcati's terse command of 'Quiet – please!'

A female voice sang the Irving Berlin song.

'I'll be loving you – always.

With a love that's true – always.

When the things you've planned

Need a helping hand,

I shall understand – always . . .'

Presently, after wandering about a little in the gloomy light, Madame Arcati drew up a stool and sat at the table between Charles and Ruth Condomine. The gramophone record came to an end. There was a deathly silence in the room.

'Is there anyone there?' Madame Arcati asked.

After a long pause, she repeated, 'Is there anyone there?'

She paused even longer, and then went on, 'One rap for yes, two raps for no. Now then – is there anyone there?'

After a shorter pause, the table gave a little bump.

'Oh!' Mrs Bradman exclaimed involuntarily.

'Sshhh!' the medium quietened her, before going on. 'Is that you, Daphne?' she asked.

The table gave a louder bump.

'Is your cold better, dear?' asked Madame Arcati.

The table gave two loud bumps very quickly.

'Oh, I'm so sorry,' Madame Arcati sympathised. 'Are you doing anything for it?'

The table bumped several times. 'I'm afraid she's rather fretful,' the medium explained to the assembled company.

There was a silence. Then Madame Arcati addressed Daphne again. 'Is there anyone there who wishes to speak to anyone here?' she asked.

After a pause, the table gave one bump.

'Ah! Now we're getting somewhere,' Madame Arcati exclaimed gleefully. Then she gave a sudden squeal of pain. 'No, Daphne, don't do that, dear, you're hurting me – Daphne, dear, please – Oh, oh, oh! – Be good, there's a dear child –'

Daphne must have ceased tormenting her, for the medium continued more calmly, 'You say there is someone there who wishes to speak to someone here?'

The table gave one bump.

'Is it me?' asked the medium.

The table gave two sharp bumps.

'Is it Dr Bradman?'

Two more bumps.

'Is it Mrs Bradman?'

Another two bumps.

'Is it Mrs Condomine?'

The table gave several very loud bumps, which continued until Madame Arcati shouted it down. 'Stop it, Daphne,' she commanded. 'Behave yourself! Is it Mr Condomine?'

There was dead silence for a moment, and then a very loud single bump.

'There's someone who wishes to speak to you, Mr Condomine,' Madame Arcati announced.

'Tell them to leave a message,' said Charles, at which the table began banging loudly.

'I really must ask you not to be flippant, Mr Condomine,' Madame Arcati admonished him, while Ruth added, 'Charles, how can you be so idiotic? You'll spoil everything.'

'I'm sorry,' Charles apologised. 'It just slipped out.'

Madame Arcati took a deep breath. 'Do you know anybody who has passed over recently?' she asked Charles.

'Not recently,' he replied, 'except perhaps my cousin in the civil service, and he wouldn't be likely to want to communicate with me. We haven't spoken for years.'

'Are you Mr Condomine's cousin in the civil service?' Madame Arcati shouted somewhat hysterically.

The table bumped violently several times.

'I'm afraid we've drawn a blank,' the medium confessed. 'Can't you think of anyone else?' she asked Charles. 'Rack your brains, Mr Condomine.'

Charles shook his head, but Ruth contributed helpfully, 'It might be old Mrs Plummett.' She looked at Charles. 'You know – she died on Whit Monday –'

Charles looked blank. 'I can't imagine why old Mrs Plummett should wish to talk to me,' he told his wife. 'We had very little in common.'

'It's worth trying, anyhow,' Ruth insisted.

Madame Arcati nodded vigorously. 'Are you old Mrs Plummett?' she asked.

The table remained still.

'She was very deaf,' Ruth recalled. 'Perhaps you'd better shout.'

The medium obliged. 'Are you old Mrs Plummett?' she shouted.

Nothing happened.

The medium shook her head in disappointment. 'There's nobody there at all,' she exclaimed.

'How very disappointing,' Mrs Bradman murmured. 'Just as we were getting on so nicely.'

'Violet, be quiet,' her husband admonished her.

Madame Arcati rose from the table. 'Well,' she announced, 'I'm afraid there's nothing for it but for me to go into a trance.' She looked around at them all. 'I had hoped to avoid it, because it's so exhausting,' she explained. 'However, what must be must be. Excuse me for a moment while I start the gramophone again.'

She went over to the gramophone, and was about to activate it when Charles called to her in a strained voice. 'Not "Always",' he requested. 'Please don't play "Always".'

'Why ever not, Charles?' his wife asked him. 'Don't be absurd. Madame Arcati knows what she's doing.'

'I'm afraid I must play it,' Madame Arcati explained

62

gently to him. 'It would be imprudent to changes horses in midstream, if you know what I mean.'

She restarted the gramophone, and Charles, shrugging his shoulders, muttered, 'Very well, have it your own way.'

Madame Arcati began to moan, then came back slowly to her stool at the end of the table and sat. After no more than a moment or two of 'Always', a child's voice could be heard, reciting rather breathlessly, 'Little Tommy Tucker sang for his supper –'

'That's Daphne, I suppose,' Dr Bradman commented. 'She ought to have had her adenoids out.'

'George – please,' his wife began, when suddenly Madame Arcati gave a loud scream, and fell off her stool onto the floor.

'Good God!' Charles exclaimed in alarm, rising from his chair. Dr Bradman also seemed disturbed by the medium's physical collapse.

'Keep still, Charles,' his wife ordered. Charles subsided, and everyone sat in tense silence for a moment. Then, suddenly, the table started bouncing about.

'It's trying to get away,' Mrs Bradman gasped. 'I can't hold it.'

'Press down hard,' Ruth told her.

The table fell over with a crash. 'There, now!' Ruth cried in dismay.

'Ought we to pick it up, or leave it where it is?' Mrs

Bradman wondered aloud, to which her husband replied irritably, 'How the hell do I know?'

'There's no need to snap at me,' Mrs Bradman complained.

After the briefest of pauses, Charles Condomine suddenly called out, 'Who said that?'

'Who said what?' Ruth asked him.

Charles looked intently at his wife. ' Didn't you hear it?' he asked, sounding alarmed. 'I heard somebody say "Leave it where it is." It was a woman's voice.'

'Nonsense, dear,' said Ruth.

'But I heard it distinctly,' Charles insisted.

'Well, nobody else did – did they?' Ruth asked, looking around the table for confirmation.

Mrs Bradman shook her head. 'I never heard a sound,' she answered.

Charles turned to his wife. 'It must have been you, Ruth,' he accused her. 'You're playing tricks on me.'

'I'm not doing anything of the sort,' Ruth replied vehemently. 'I have not uttered at all.'

There was another pause. Then Charles, by now extremely agitated, shouted, 'Ventriloquism – that's what it is. Ventriloquism!'

'What's the matter with you?' Ruth asked him, irritably.

'You must have heard what she said just then,' Charles exclaimed, addressing them all. 'At least one of you must have heard that.'

They all looked perplexed. 'Heard what?' asked Ruth.

Charles looked at the others in consternation. 'It was a woman's voice,' he told them. 'She said "Good evening, Charles."'

When no one responded, he addressed them all with urgency in his voice. 'Do you mean to sit there solemnly,' he asked, 'and tell me that none of you heard anything at all?'

'I certainly didn't,' Dr Bradman assured him.

'Neither did I,' added the doctor's wife. 'I – I wish I had. I should love to have heard something.'

Ruth now rounded on her husband. 'It is you who are playing tricks, Charles,' she accused him. 'You're acting to try and frighten us, and I don't –'

'I'm not,' Charles interrupted her breathlessly. 'I swear I'm not.' He turned his head suddenly, as though listening to something, and then, after a few moments, asked intensely, 'Who are you?'

He must have received, or imagined he received, an answer, for he rose suddenly from the table, and strode about the room. 'I can't bear this for another minute,' he shouted. 'Get up, everybody. The entertainment's over.'

He rushed across the room and switched on the lights.

Chapter Five

General confusion ensued. 'What's happening?' Mrs Bradman cried, while Ruth complained angrily, 'Oh, Charles, how tiresome of you. Just as we were beginning to enjoy ourselves.'

Charles shook his head vehemently. 'Never again – that's all that I can say,' he told her. 'Never, never again, as long as I live.'

'But what on earth's the matter with you?' Ruth pleaded.

'Nothing's the matter with me,' Charles insisted. 'I'm just sick of the whole business, that's all.'

'Did you hear anything that we didn't hear, really?' Dr Bradman asked him.

With a forced laugh, Charles replied, 'Of course not – I was only pretending.'

'I know you were,' Ruth chimed in. 'And what's more –'

She was interrupted by Mrs Bradman who cried out, pointing at the floor, 'Oh dear – look at Madame Arcati.'

The medium was lying on the floor with her feet up on the stool from which she had fallen. She was obviously quite unconscious. One of her shoes lay on the floor, and her scarf was alarmingly tight around her throat. Except for the quivering of her hands, she would have seemed dead.

Ruth looked concerned. 'What are we going to do with her?' she asked.

'Bring her round,' said Charles fiercely. 'Bring her back to consciousness as soon as possible.'

Dr Bradman went over and knelt down beside Madame Arcati. He felt her pulse, and then said, 'She'll be all right. I think we'd better leave her alone.'

'But she might stay like that for hours,' Ruth complained.

After examining the medium's eyes, Dr Bradman observed, 'She's out all right. And I can't be sure for how long.'

'Bring her round,' Charles cried again, almost hysterically. 'It's dangerous to leave her like that.' He turned to Dr Bradman. 'You're a doctor,' he said. 'Do something.'

'Really, Charles,' Ruth exclaimed, 'you are behaving most peculiarly.'

Charles now knelt beside Madame Arcati and shook her violently. 'Wake up, Madame Arcati,' he shouted. 'Wake up! It's time to go home.'

'Here, go easy, old man,' Dr Bradman cautioned him, continuing to examine his unexpected patient.

'Get some brandy,' Charles ordered, now taking control. 'Give her some brandy. Lift her into the chair. Help me, Bradman.'

While Ruth went to the drinks table and poured out a large glass of brandy, Charles and Dr Bradman lifted Madame Arcati laboriously from the floor, Mrs Bradman taking the stool from under the medium's feet and placing it back at the piano. Madame Arcati was put in an armchair where she remained slumped and still unconscious.

Leaning over her, Charles went on shouting urgently, 'Wake up, Madame Arcati – Little Tommy Tucker, Madame Arcati!'

Ruth came over to them. 'Here's the brandy,' she said. Charles took the glass from her and administered a sip to Madame Arcati, while Dr Bradman patted the medium's hand. She gave a slight moan, and shivered as Charles forced brandy between her lips, still calling 'Wake up, Madame Arcati!'

Madame Arcati opened her eyes, and looked curiously about her. 'Well, that's that,' she observed, sounding quite placid and unconcerned, as though nothing untoward had occurred.

'Are you all right?' Ruth asked her solicitously.

'Certainly I am,' Madame Arcati replied with vigour. 'Never felt better in my life.'

'Would you like some more brandy?' Charles asked her, bottle in hand.

Madame Arcati looked up at him. 'So that's the funny taste in my mouth,' she said, sounding quite annoyed. 'Well, really!' She focused her glance on the doctor. 'Fancy allowing them to give me brandy, Dr Bradman. You ought to have known better. Brandy on top of a trance might have been catastrophic.' She looked up at Charles. 'Take it away, please,' she requested firmly. 'I probably shan't sleep a wink tonight as it is.'

'I know I shan't,' Charles muttered, as he snatched the brandy glass from Dr Bradman.

'Why on earth not?' Ruth asked him.

Charles walked over to the mantelpiece, got rid of the brandy glass, and took a cigarette, before replying in a pathetic voice, 'The whole experience has completely unhinged me.'

Madame Arcati looked around her. 'Well, what happened?' she asked the room in general. 'Was it satisfactory?'

'Nothing much happened, Madame Arcati, after you went off into your trance,' Ruth told her with a shrug of the shoulders.

The medium shook her head vigorously. 'Something happened all right,' she insisted. 'I can feel it.'

She rose from her chair, went over to the fireplace and sniffed. 'No poltergeist, at any rate,' she exclaimed, looking pleased. 'That's a good thing, at least.' She turned to face the others. 'Any apparitions?' she asked.

'Not a thing,' said Dr Bradman, sadly.

Madame Arcati's visage now wore an almost incredulous expression. 'That's very curious,' she said. 'I feel as though something tremendous has taken place.'

'Well, Charles pretended he heard a voice, in order to frighten us,' Ruth admitted. 'But that was all.'

'It was only a joke,' Charles protested, attempting a throwaway tone.

'A very poor one, if I may say so,' the medium told him sharply. She moved around the room, looking in all directions, prodding cushions and moving vases and ashtrays that caught her attention. She took a particularly careful peek under the table used for the seance. 'A very poor joke indeed,' she repeated. 'Nevertheless, I am prepared to swear that there is someone else in this room apart from us.'

'I don't see how there can be, really, Madame Arcati,' Ruth protested.

The medium now wore a worried expression. 'I do hope I haven't gone and released something,' she exclaimed. She paused momentarily, then shrugged her shoulders. 'Well, in any case,' she continued, 'we are bound to find out within a day or two.' She turned to the Condomines. 'If any manifestation should occur, or you hear any unexpected noises, you might let me know at once.'

'Of course we will,' Ruth promised her. 'We'll telephone you immediately.'

Madame Arcati nodded her head, seemingly satisfied with this assurance. 'Well, I think I really must be on my way now,' she told Ruth.

'Wouldn't you like anything before you go?' Ruth enquired politely. 'Some tea or coffee perhaps?'

'No, thank you, Mrs Condomine,' was the reply. 'I have some Ovaltine all ready in a saucepan at home. It only needs hotting up.'

'Would you like to leave your bicycle here, and let us drive you?' Dr Bradman suggested. His wife added, 'I honestly do think you should, Madame Arcati, after that trance and everything. You can't be feeling quite yourself.'

'Nonsense, my dear, I'm as fit as a fiddle,' the medium assured her. 'I always feel absolutely capital after a trance. It really does rejuvenate me.' She turned to Ruth. 'Goodnight, Mrs Condomine,' she said.

'It was awfully sweet of you to take so much trouble,' Ruth thanked her as they shook hands.

'I'm only sorry that so little occurred,' the medium replied with an apologetic smile. 'It's that cold of Daphne's, I expect.' She gave a vigorous shake of the head. 'You know what children are like when they have anything wrong with them. We must try again, some other evening.'

'That would be lovely,' Ruth assured her politely.

Madame Arcati then shook hands with the doctor's wife and said goodnight to her, to which Mrs Bradman responded by telling her, gushingly, 'It was thrilling, it really was! I felt the table shaking under my hands.'

When Madame Arcati shook hands with Dr Bradman and said goodnight, he replied suavely, 'Congratulations, Madame Arcati.'

She looked at him up and down, coldly. 'I am fully aware of the irony in your voice, Dr Bradman,' she told him. 'As a matter of fact, you'd be an admirable subject for telepathic hypnosis. A great friend of mine is an expert in that. I should like her to look you over.'

The doctor gave her a slight bow. 'I'm sure I would be charmed,' he said.

Madame Arcati strode to the door. 'Goodnight, everyone,' she called, as Charles opened the door for her. 'Next time, we must really put our backs into it.'

With a final comprehensive smile and a wave of the hand, she went out, followed by Charles who, carrying her cloak, escorted her to her bicycle, and began to help her light her safety lamp.

Inside, Ruth sank down onto the sofa, laughing helplessly. 'Oh dear! – Oh dear!' she gasped, while Dr Bradman picked up the seance table and moved it away from the centre of the room, then put the desk chair back to its original position, and did the same with the pouffe.

Mrs Bradman, beginning to laugh too, warned Ruth, 'Be careful, Mrs Condomine. She might still be able to hear you. She has extraordinary powers, after all.'

'I can't help it,' Ruth replied through her laughter. 'I really can't. I've been holding this in for ages.'

'She certainly put you in your place, George,' Mrs Bradman said to her husband. 'And it serves you right.'

'She's raving mad, of course – mad as a hatter,' said Ruth.

'But do you think she really believes all of that?' Mrs Bradman asked.

'Of course not,' said Dr Bradman. 'The whole thing's a put-up job.' He gave a little laugh. 'I must say, though, that she shoots a more original line than they generally do.'

'Yes,' Ruth agreed, nodding her head. 'I should think that she's probably half convinced herself by now.'

'Yes, quite possible,' the doctor said.' Actually, her trance was genuine enough – but that, of course, is easily accounted for.'

'Do you mean it's sheer hysteria?' Ruth asked him.

'Yes – a form of hysteria, I should imagine,' the doctor replied.

His wife smiled at Ruth. 'I do hope Mr Condomine

got all the atmosphere he wanted for his book,' she said. 'After all, that's what it was all about, this evening.'

Ruth nodded. 'He might have got a good deal more if he hadn't spoiled everything by showing off,' she exclaimed. 'I'm really very cross with him.'

She paused and gave a slight shiver. 'I suddenly felt a draught, just then,' she said. 'There must be a window open.'

Dr Bradman looked around at the windows. 'No,' he assured her, 'they're all shut.'

Mrs Bradman laughed. 'Perhaps it was one of those what-do-you-call'ems that Madame Arcati was talking about.'

'Elementals,' said the doctor.

Ruth began to laugh again. 'Oh no, it couldn't be,' she gasped. 'She distinctly said that it was the wrong time of the year for Elementals.'

Charles now came back into the room. 'Well, the old girl's gone pedalling off down the drive at a hell of a speed with her safety lamp glowing in the moonlight. We had a bit of trouble lighting the lamp.'

'Poor thing,' Mrs Bradman gasped, still laughing helplessly.

Charles, however, looked serious. 'I've got a theory about her, you know,' he informed them all. 'I believe she is completely sincere.'

'Charles!' his wife expostulated. 'How could she be?'

Charles Condomine addressed Dr Bradman. 'Wouldn't that be possible, Doctor?' he asked. 'Some form of self-hypnotism?'

Dr Bradman considered for a moment before replying. Then he began to speak cautiously. 'It might be,' he said. 'As I started to explain to your wife just now, there are certain types of hysterical subjects that –'

Mrs Bradman interrupted him. 'George, dear, it's getting terribly late,' she announced, pointing to her watch. 'We really must go home. You have to get up so early in the morning.'

'You see?' the doctor exclaimed in mock dismay. 'The moment I begin to talk about anything that really interests me, my wife interrupts me with –'

'You know I'm right, darling,' Mrs Bradman told him. 'It's past eleven.'

Dr Bradman gave a reluctant nod of the head. 'I'll do a little reading-up on the whole business,' he said, addressing Charles Condomine. 'Just for the fun of it.'

'You really must have a drink before you go,' Charles invited him, but the doctor replied, 'No, really, thank you. Violet's quite right, I'm afraid. I do have to get up abominably early tomorrow morning. I have a patient being operated on in Canterbury.'

Mrs Bradman went over to Ruth, who rose from the sofa.

'It has been a thrilling evening,' the doctor's wife told her hostess. 'I'm sure I shall never forget it. It was so sweet of you to include us.'

'Indeed, yes. Goodnight, Mrs Condomine,' Dr Bradman added. 'Thank you so much.'

'You're sure about the drink?' Charles asked him, pouring a brandy for himself as he spoke.

'Quite sure, thanks,' the doctor replied.

'We'll let you know if we find any poltergeists whirling about,' Ruth promised the Bradmans with a laugh.

'I should never forgive you if you didn't,' Dr Bradman replied, joining in her laughter.

The doctor's wife was already at the door. 'Come along, darling,' she called.

They left, with Charles following them out of the door. Ruth went over to the piano, got herself a cigarette and lit it, and then went to lean against the fireplace as Charles came back into the room.

'Well?' Ruth asked, as she went to the windows to draw the curtains completely, giving the room a more intimate atmosphere.

'Well?' Charles echoed her absently.

Ruth expanded her query. 'Would you say the evening had been profitable?'

'Yes – I suppose so,' Charles replied.

'I must say it was extremely funny at times,' Ruth observed.

'Yes – it certainly was,' Charles replied, still sounding preoccupied.

Ruth looked at him for a few moments before asking, 'Charles, do tell me. What's the matter?'

'The matter?'

'Yes. You seem odd, somehow,' she told him. 'Are you sure you feel quite well?'

Charles made an attempt to pull himself together. 'Perfectly, darling,' he assured her. 'But I think I'll have another drink.'

He went across to the drinks table and began to mix himself another brandy and soda. 'Do you want one?' he asked Ruth.

'No, thank you, Charles,' she replied, watching him with some concern.

'It's rather chilly in this room,' Charles complained as he sipped his drink.

'Come over by the fire, then,' Ruth said gently.

'I don't think I'll make any notes tonight – I'll start fresh in the morning,' Charles said as he turned, glass in hand. Suddenly he stopped, stared, and dropped his glass, spilling its contents on the floor. 'My God!' he cried.

What had startled him was that he imagined he saw a young woman sitting on a chair against the wall, a slight smile on her face. She was charmingly dressed in a kind of negligee, and looked beautiful, except that everything about her – her hair, her skin, her hands, her dress – was grey. She looked as though she were not quite of this world.

'That was very clumsy of you, Charles,' his wife exclaimed. However, he paid no attention to her. His eyes were still focused on the apparition, if that was what it was. 'Elvira!' he cried, 'Then it's true. It *was* you!'

The image spoke, or at least Charles imagined that it did. 'Of course it was me, Charles.'

Ruth came over to her husband, looking extremely concerned. 'Charles, what are you talking about?' she asked him.

Ignoring Ruth, and still staring at the apparition, Charles whispered, 'Are you a ghost?'

'I suppose I must be – it's all very confusing,' the young woman said. At least, Charles imagined that she spoke, for Ruth appeared to hear nothing.

Becoming even more agitated, Ruth came up close to her husband. 'Charles,' she exhorted him, 'what do you keep looking over there for? Look at me. What's happened?'

'Don't you see?' asked Charles, his body rigid, his eyes still fixed on the other side of the room.

'See what?' Ruth asked him, now in a state of extreme agitation.

'Elvira. Elvira, my first wife. Elvira. There she is,' said Charles, gesturing to the other side of the room.

Ruth followed his gaze, but could see nothing out of the

ordinary. She stared at him incredulously. 'Elvira?' she gasped.

'Yes. Elvira,' Charles repeated. Then, with a courageous effort at social grace, he added, 'Elvira, dear, this is Ruth, Ruth, this is Elvira.'

Chapter Six

———

A pregnant silence followed Charles's desperate attempt to introduce his present wife to his dead former wife. Ruth looked at him intently, and then tried to take his arm. 'Come and sit down, Charles,' she urged him with forced calmness.

Charles, however, moved away from her, stepping over the brandy glass. 'Do you mean to say you can't see Elvira?' he asked.

Ruth took a deep breath. 'Listen, Charles,' she replied. 'You just sit down quietly by the fire and I'll mix you another drink. Don't worry about the mess on the carpet – Edith can clean it up in the morning.'

She tried to take him by the arm again, but he broke away from her. 'You must be able to see Elvira,' he insisted. 'She's there – look – right in front of you – there –'

'Are you mad?' cried Ruth, desperately. 'What's happened to you, Charles?'

'You can't see Elvira? You really can't see her?' Charles asked, incredulously, pointing at where he was seeing the apparition.

'If this is a joke, Charles, it's gone quite far enough,' Ruth told him firmly. 'Now, sit down, for God's sake, and don't be so idiotic.'

Charles clutched his head in despair. 'What am I to do?' he cried. 'What the hell am I to do?'

Unheard, of course, by Ruth, Elvira's apparition spoke to Charles. 'I think you might at least be a little more pleased to see me,' she said. 'After all, you conjured me up.'

'I didn't do any such thing,' Charles replied, extremely cross at the suggestion.

'Nonsense. Of course you did,' he heard Elvira say. 'That awful child with the cold came and told me you wanted to see me urgently.'

'It was all a mistake,' Charles shouted at her. 'A horrible mistake.'

'Stop shouting like that, Charles,' Ruth ordered him, she herself shouting at the top of her voice. 'I've told you before, the joke's gone far enough.'

Charles groaned in despair. 'I've gone mad, that's what it is,' he cried. 'I've just gone stark, raving mad.'

Ruth poured out another brandy, and brought it to him. 'Here – drink this,' she ordered.

Charles took the glass from her, mechanically. 'This is appalling,' he gasped, hardly noticing his wife's action.

'Do try to relax,' Ruth implored him.

'How can I relax?' he asked her, pathetically. 'I shall never be able to relax again as long as I live.'

'Drink some of that brandy,' Ruth ordered.

Charles did as he was told, and drank his brandy in one gulp. 'There, now – are you satisfied?' he asked Ruth fiercely. His voice was almost a scream.

'Now sit down,' said Ruth firmly.

Charles looked at her in exasperation. 'Why are you so anxious for me to sit down?' he asked. 'What good will that do?'

'I want you to relax,' Ruth explained patiently. 'You can't relax standing up.'

Charles heard Elvira's apparition say calmly, 'African natives can. They can stand on one leg for hours.'

'I don't happen to be an African native,' Charles shouted.

'You don't happen to be a *what?*' Ruth asked, puzzled, frustration growing in her voice.

'An African native,' Charles snarled at her savagely.

Ruth looked absolutely perplexed. 'What's that got to do with it?' she wanted to know.

Charles gave a weary sigh. 'It doesn't matter, Ruth. Really, it doesn't matter,' he told her. 'We'll say no more about it. Please.'

He went over to the armchair and sat, sprawled in exhaustion. 'See, I've sat down,' he pointed out to her.

'Would you like some more brandy?' Ruth asked, her voice now solicitous.

'Yes, please,' he replied promptly.

Ruth went over to the drinks table with his glass, at which Charles heard Elvira's apparition commenting, 'Very unwise, Charles. You always had a weak head.'

'I could drink you under the table,' Charles muttered.

'There's no need to be aggressive, Charles,' his present wife snapped at him. 'I'm doing my best to help you.'

Charles looked at her helplessly. 'I'm sorry,' he said.

Ruth brought his brandy across to him. 'Here,' she said coldly as she handed the glass to him. 'Drink this, and then we'll go to bed.'

'Get rid of her, and then we can talk in peace, darling. And perhaps not just talk,' Charles heard Elvira's apparition advise suggestively.

'That's a thoroughly immoral suggestion,' he replied. 'You ought to be ashamed of yourself.'

'What is there immoral in that?' Ruth wanted to know. She sounded as though she were having great difficulty in not losing her temper.

Charles shook his head wearily. 'I wasn't talking to you,' he told her.

'Who were you talking to, then?' she asked.

'Elvira, of course,' he replied in exasperation.

'To hell with Elvira!' Ruth shouted.

'There now – she's getting cross,' Charles heard Elvira's apparition say.

'I don't blame her,' he replied, at which Ruth, not surprisingly asked, 'What don't you blame her for?'

'Oh God!' Charles exclaimed despairingly.

Ruth took a deep breath. 'Now look here, Charles,' she began. 'I gather you've got some sort of plan behind all this. I'm not a complete fool. I suspected you were up to something when you were doing that idiotic seance and –'

'Don't be so silly,' Charles interrupted her, angrily. 'What plan could I possibly have?'

'I don't know,' Ruth admitted. 'But it's probably something to do with the characters in your book – how they, or one of them, would react to a certain situation.'

She wagged her finger in his face as she continued, 'Let me make this clear to you. I refuse to be used as a guinea pig unless I am warned beforehand what it's all about.'

Charles moved closer to his wife. 'Now listen carefully, Ruth,' he ordered. 'Elvira is here. She's standing just a few yards away from you.'

'Yes, of course, dear,' Ruth retorted sarcastically. 'I can see her distinctly. She's under the piano with a zebra.'

'Now, Ruth –' Charles began to protest, but she cut him short. 'I am not going to stay here arguing any longer,' she told him.

'Hurray!' Elvira's apparition shouted, to which Charles replied savagely, 'Shut up!'

Ruth was incensed. 'How dare you speak to me like that!' she screamed at him.

Charles was becoming increasingly desperate. 'Listen, Ruth – please listen,' he began, but she cut him short. 'I will not listen to any more of this nonsense,' she said coldly. 'I am going up to bed now, so I'll leave you to turn out the lights.'

She started to leave, then turned back to face Charles again. 'I shan't be asleep,' she informed him. 'I'm too upset to sleep. So you can come in and say good night to me if you feel like it.'

'That's big of her, I must say,' Elvira's apparition chortled.

'Be quiet!' Charles ordered her. 'You're behaving like a guttersnipe.'

'This guttersnipe has nothing more to say to you. Goodnight, Charles,' said Ruth icily.

She turned and walked swiftly out of the room.

Charles followed her to the door. 'Ruth –' he began, but got no further before Elvira's voice uttered again. 'That was one of the most enjoyable half-hours I have ever spent,' her voice said happily.

Charles put his glass down on the drinks table. 'Oh, Elvira,' he said, staring at her apparition, 'how could you!'

'Poor Ruth!' Elvira chortled.

Charles continued to stare at her, still hardly able to believe his eyes. 'This is obviously some kind of hallucination, isn't it? he asked.

'I'm afraid I don't know the technical term for it,' Elvira replied.

Charles wrung his hands in despair. 'What am I going to do?' he wailed.

'Do what Ruth suggested,' Elvira advised him. 'Relax.'

He gave a sigh, paused, and then asked her, 'Where have you come from?'

Elvira thought for a moment before replying. Then, with a shake of the head, she said, 'Do you know, it's very peculiar, but I've sort of forgotten.'

'Are you here indefinitely?' he asked her, cautiously.

'I'm afraid I don't know that either,' she confessed.

'Oh, my God!' Charles muttered in despair.

'Why do you need to know?' Elvira asked him. 'Would you hate it so much if I were to be here indefinitely?'

'Well, you must admit it would be embarrassing,' he replied.

'I don't see why, really,' Elvira insisted. 'It's all just a question of adjusting yourself.' She pouted. 'Anyhow,' she went on, I think it's horrid of you to be so unwelcoming and disagreeable.'

'Now look here, Elvira –' Charles began, but Elvira, now close to tears, interrupted him. 'I really do think it's horrid of you,' she cried. 'I think you're being terribly mean.'

Attempting not to sound exasperated, Charles said, 'Try to see my side of it, dear. I've been married to Ruth for five years, and you've been "dead" for seven –'

'Not dead, Charles,' she corrected him. 'Passed over. It's considered vulgar to say "dead" where I come from.'

'Passed over, then,' Charles sighed.

'At any rate,' Elvira went on, 'now that I'm here, the least you can do is make a pretence of being amiable about it –'

'Of course, my dear, I'm delighted in one way,' Charles attempted to assure her, but before he could continue Elvira sobbed, 'I don't believe you love me any more.'

'I shall always love the memory of you,' Charles told her.

Elvira approached him slowly. 'You mustn't think me unreasonable,' she said, trying not to give way to tears, 'but I really am more than a little hurt. You called me back – at great inconvenience I came – and you've been thoroughly churlish ever since I arrived.'

'Believe me, Elvira,' Charles said gently, 'I most emphatically did not send for you. There's been some mistake.'

'Well, somebody asked for me,' Elvira replied irritably,

'and that horrid child said it was you. I remember I was playing backgammon with a very sweet old oriental gentleman – I think his name was Genghis Khan – and I'd just thrown double sixes, and then the wretched child paged me, and the next thing I knew I was in this room.' She paused. 'Perhaps it was your subconscious that asked for me, Charles,' she suggested.

Charles looked annoyed at this. 'You must simply find out whether you are going to stay or not,' he told her, 'and then we can make arrangements accordingly.'

'I don't see how I can possibly find out,' Elvira insisted.

'Well, try to think,' he suggested. 'Isn't there anyone that you know, anyone that you can get in touch with over there – on the other side, or whatever it's called – who could advise you?'

Elvira shook her head. 'I can't think of anyone,' she murmured. 'It all seems so far away – as though I'd dreamed it –'

'You must know somebody else there besides Genghis Khan,' Charles exclaimed irritably.

'Oh, Charles,' she murmured, and then paused.

'What is it?' he asked.

'I want to cry,' Elvira said, 'but I don't think I'm able to –'

'What do you want to cry for?' he snapped irritably.

'It's seeing you again,' she told him, 'and you being so irascible, like you always used to be –'

'I don't mean to be irascible, Elvira –' he began.

'Darling, I don't mind really,' she interrupted him hastily. 'I never did.'

They looked at each other in silence for a moment. Then Charles asked, 'Is it cold? – being a ghost, I mean.'

Elvira paused in thought, before replying, 'No – I don't think so.'

'What happens if I touch you?' Charles wanted to know.

Elvira shook her head. 'I doubt if you can,' she replied. 'Do you want to?'

Charles went to the sofa and sat. 'Oh, Elvira,' he cried, burying his face in his hands.

She came over to the sofa. 'What is it, darling?' she asked.

He looked up at her. 'I really do feel strange, seeing you again,' he confessed.

'That's better,' she exclaimed.

'What's better?' he asked.

'Your voice was kinder,' she told him.

He continued to look at her. 'Was I ever unkind to you when you were alive?' he asked.

Elvira laughed. 'Of course you were. Often!'

Charles looked affronted. 'Oh, how can you say that, Elvira?' he demanded. 'I'm sure that's an exaggeration.'

'Not at all,' she insisted. 'You were an absolute pig that

time we went to Cornwall and stayed in a perfectly awful hotel. You hit me with a billiard cue –'

'Only very, very gently,' Charles insisted.

Elvira came close to the sofa. 'I loved you so very much,' she murmured softly.

'I loved you too,' Charles replied. He put out a hand and tried to touch her, but then drew his hand away. 'No, I can't touch you,' he exclaimed. 'Isn't that horrible?'

'Perhaps it's as well, if I'm going to stay for any length of time,' Elvira observed. She sat on an arm of the sofa, close to him, and turned off the lamp next to them, leaving just the warm glow of the dying embers in the fireplace to illuminate the room.

'I suppose I shall wake up eventually,' Charles murmured, 'but I feel strangely peaceful now.'

'That's right, darling,' Elvira assured him. 'Put your head back.'

He did as he was told. 'Like that?'

Elvira stroked his hair. 'Can you feel anything?' she asked him.

'Only a very little breeze through my hair,' he replied.

'Well, that's better than nothing,' she told him.

'I suppose if I'm really out of my mind, they'll put me in an asylum,' Charles murmured drowsily.

'Don't worry about that, darling,' Elvira whispered. 'Just relax.'

'Poor Ruth,' Charles murmured, now sounding very drowsy indeed.

'To hell with Ruth,' Elvira said sweetly, as she continued gently to stroke his hair.

Chapter Seven

——▬——

When Ruth Condomine came into the sitting room the next morning at about nine-thirty, the sun was pouring in through the open French windows, and Edith had already set the breakfast table for two, and placed the morning newspaper on it, along with a pot of hot coffee. Ruth took a seat at the table, poured herself some coffee, and then picked up *The Times*, which she began to read while waiting for Edith to bring in the breakfast.

She was yawning over the editorial page when the door opened and Charles entered the room. Going across to Ruth, he kissed her on the cheek and greeted her jovially with 'Good morning, darling.'

It was with a certain stiffness that Ruth replied, 'Good morning, Charles.'

Charles went over to the open window and took a deep breath. 'It certainly is,' he exclaimed, sounding extremely happy.

'What certainly is what?' Ruth asked him, frigidly.

'A good morning,' he told her, beaming. 'A tremendously good morning.' Looking out of the window, he continued cheerfully, 'There isn't a cloud in the sky, and everything looks newly washed.'

Ruth made no comment on this, but turned a page of her newspaper. 'Edith should be ready to bring our breakfast in by now,' she said. 'You'd better ring for her.'

Charles went over to the mantelpiece and rang a bell. 'Anything interesting in *The Times*?' he asked.

'Don't be silly, Charles,' Ruth replied dismissively, as though it were a completely ridiculous question.

Charles sat at the table with her, and poured himself some coffee. 'I intend to work all day,' he announced happily.

'Good,' Ruth replied, still sounding quite curt.

'It's extraordinary about daylight, isn't it?' Charles exclaimed, taking a sip of his coffee.

'How do you mean?' Ruth was curious to know.

'I mean the way it reduces everything to normal,' Charles explained.

'Does it?' Ruth's tone was now quite frigid.

'Yes – it does,' Charles stated firmly.

'I'm sure I'm very glad to hear it,' she replied.

Charles looked upset. 'You're very glacial this morning, Ruth,' he complained.

'Are you surprised?' asked Ruth.

'Frankly – yes,' he told her. 'I expected more of you.'

'Well, really!' Ruth exclaimed with indignation.

'I've always looked upon you as a woman of perception and understanding,' Charles continued.

Ruth glared at him. 'Then you'd better consider this one of my off days,' she announced truculently.

Edith suddenly came into the room with a tray holding bacon and eggs and toast, which she brought over to the breakfast table. 'Good morning, ma'am, good morning, sir,' she greeted them as she served the food.

Ruth merely nodded in reply, but Charles beamed at the maid and greeted her boisterously with 'Good morning, Edith, my dear.'

'Good morning, sir,' the maid repeated.

'Feeling fit, Edith?' Charles asked her.

'Yes, sir. Thank you, sir,' she replied.

'How's cook this morning?' Charles enquired, still sounding extremely ebullient.

The maid looked surprised. 'I don't know, sir,' she answered. 'I haven't asked her.'

'You should,' Charles instructed her. 'You should begin every day by asking everyone how they are. It oils the wheels.'

'Yes, sir,' Edith replied submissively.

'Greet her from me, will you?' Charles requested.

'Yes, sir,' Edith repeated.

Ruth thought it time to bring her husband's cheerful banter to an end. 'That will be all for the moment, Edith,' she told the maid, who murmured 'Yes'm' and left the room at her usual high speed.

'I wish you wouldn't be so facetious with the servants, Charles,' Ruth complained. 'It simply confuses them and undermines their morale.'

Charles gave her a look of mock disapproval. 'I consider that point of view retrogressive, if not downright feudal,' he exclaimed.

'I don't care what you consider it,' Ruth snapped. 'I have to run the house, and you don't.'

'Are you implying that I couldn't?' Charles wanted to know.

Ruth grunted. 'You're certainly at liberty to try,' she told him.

Charles took a deep breath. 'I take back what I said about it being a good morning,' he observed. 'In fact, it's a perfectly horrid morning.'

Ruth chose to ignore this. 'You'd better eat your breakfast while it's hot,' she advised, pointing at his food.

'It isn't hot,' he replied sulkily.

Ruth put down her copy of *The Times*, and addressed

him in anger. 'Now look here, Charles,' she exclaimed. 'In your younger days, this display of roguish flippancy might have been alluring, but in a middle-aged novelist it's simply nauseating.'

Charles gazed at her blandly. 'Would you like me to writhe at your feet in a frenzy of self-abasement?' he asked.

'That would be equally nauseating,' his wife replied, 'but, under the circumstances, certainly a great deal more appropriate.'

Charles sighed. 'I really don't see what I've done that's so awful,' he complained.

'You behaved abominably last night,' Ruth told him. 'You wounded me and insulted me.'

'I was the victim of an aberration,' Charles began to explain, but Ruth interrupted him with 'Nonsense! You were extremely drunk.'

'Drunk?' Charles sounded surprised.

'You had four strong Martinis before dinner,' Ruth reminded him. 'Then you followed them with a great deal too much Burgundy at dinner, and heaven knows how much port and kummel with Dr Bradman while I was doing my best to entertain that mad Arcati woman. And then you had several double brandies later – I gave them to you myself. Of course you were drunk.'

Charles glared at her. 'So that's your story, is it?' he asked, sounding affronted.

Ruth regarded him steadily. 'You refused to come to bed,' she pointed out, 'and finally, when I came down at three in the morning to see what had happened to you, I found you in an alcoholic coma on the sofa, with your hair all over your face. The fire had gone out and the room was freezing.'

'I was not in the least drunk, Ruth,' Charles asserted firmly. Then, adopting a more reasonable tone, he continued, 'Something happened to me last night. Something very peculiar happened to me.'

'Nonsense,' Ruth snorted dismissively.

'It isn't nonsense,' he insisted. 'I know it seems like nonsense now, in the clear and remorseless light of day, but last night it was far from being nonsense. I honestly had some sort of hallucination –'

'I would really much rather not discuss it any further,' Ruth interrupted him coldly.

'But you must discuss it – please,' Charles pleaded. 'It's very disturbing.'

'There I agree with you,' Ruth replied swiftly. 'It showed you up in the most unpleasant light. And I find *that* extremely disturbing.'

Charles faced her squarely, and took a deep breath. 'Ruth, I swear to you,' he told her earnestly, 'that during the seance I was convinced that I heard Elvira's voice.'

Ruth remained unconvinced. 'Nobody else did,' she pointed out.

'I can't help that,' Charles persisted. 'I did.'

'But you couldn't have,' said Ruth, sounding exasperated.

Charles ignored her contradiction. 'And later on, I was equally convinced that she was in this room,' he continued. 'I saw her distinctly, and I talked to her. In fact, after you'd gone to bed we had quite a cosy little chat.'

Ruth gave a tight smile. 'And do you seriously expect me to believe that you weren't drunk?' she asked derisively.

'I *know* I wasn't drunk,' Charles insisted with vehemence. 'If I'd been all that drunk, I should have a dreadful hangover now, shouldn't I?'

'I'm not at all sure that you haven't,' Ruth replied.

'I haven't got the slightest trace of a headache,' Charles assured her. 'And my tongue's not coated. Here, look at it.' He put out his tongue for her to inspect.

'I've not the least desire to look at your tongue,' Ruth informed him coldly. 'Kindly put it in again.'

Charles got up, went to the mantelpiece, and lit a cigarette. 'I know what it is,' he exclaimed. 'You're frightened.'

'Frightened!' Ruth expostulated. 'Rubbish. What is there for me to be frightened of?'

'You're frightened of Elvira,' Charles told her. 'You wouldn't have minded that much, even if I had been drunk. It's only because it was all mixed up with Elvira.'

Ruth flashed her derisive smile again. 'I seem to remember

last night before dinner telling you that your views of female psychology were rather didactic,' she reminded him. 'I was right. I should have added that they were puerile.'

Charles wagged a finger at her. 'That was when it all began,' he exclaimed.

'When all what began?' Ruth asked, impatiently.

Charles moved over to the sofa, trying to recall in accurate detail the events of the previous evening. 'We were talking far too much about Elvira,' he reminded Ruth. 'It's dangerous to have somebody strongly in your mind when you start dabbling with the occult in a seance.'

'She certainly wasn't strongly in my mind,' Ruth asserted, obviously put out at the suggestion.

'Well, she was in mine,' Charles felt obliged to confess.

'Oh, she was, was she?' Ruth snapped belligerently.

Charles came over to the breakfast table and stood facing his wife. 'You tried to make me say that Elvira was more physically attractive than you,' he reminded her. 'You tried to make me say that, so that you could hold it over me in the future.'

'I did not,' Ruth declared with some passion. 'I don't give a hoot how physically attractive she was.'

'Oh, yes, you do,' Charles insisted. 'Your whole being is devoured with jealousy.'

Ruth got up from the table, and strode across the room. 'This is too much!' she exclaimed indignantly.

'Women!' Charles shouted, flinging himself into the armchair. 'My God, what I think of women!'

'Your view of women is academic, to say the least of it,' Ruth sneered. 'Just because you've always been dominated by them, it doesn't necessarily follow that you know anything about them.'

'I've never been dominated by anyone,' Charles retorted with a superior smile.

Ruth went back to the breakfast table. 'You were hagridden by your mother until you were twenty-three,' she told Charles. 'And then you got into the clutches of that awful Mrs whatever-her-name-was –'

'Mrs Winthrop-Llewellyn,' Charles contributed helpfully.

'I'm not interested in her name,' Elvira continued, as she cleared the plates from the breakfast table, working her way around it with her back to Charles. 'Then there was Elvira,' she recalled. 'Elvira, who ruled you with a rod of iron.'

Charles shook his head dismissively. 'Elvira never ruled anyone,' he insisted. 'She was much too elusive.' He paused for a moment in contemplation of his first wife. 'That was one of her greatest charms,' he recalled.

Ruth chose to ignore this. 'Then there was Maud Charteris –' she continued.

'My affair with Maud Charteris lasted exactly seven and a half weeks,' Charles corrected her. 'And I seem to remember she cried all the time.'

'That was her way of dominating you – it's called the tyranny of tears,' Ruth pointed out. 'And then there was –'

Charles had clearly had enough of this. 'If you wish to make an inventory of my sex life, dear,' he interrupted her in his sweetest voice, 'I think it only fair to tell you that you've missed out several interesting episodes. I'll consult my diary and give you the complete list after lunch.'

'It's no use trying to impress me with your routine amorous exploits,' Ruth retorted sharply.

'Actually, the only woman in my entire life who has ever attempted to dominate me is you,' Charles barked at her. 'You've been at it for years.'

'That is completely untrue,' Ruth insisted indignantly.

'Oh no, it isn't,' he declared. 'You boss me and bully me and order me about all the time. You won't even allow me to have an hallucination if I want to.'

Ruth came over to her husband and regarded him seriously. 'Charles,' she said, speaking slowly and emphatically, 'alcohol will ruin your whole life if you allow it to get hold of you, you know.'

Charles now looked completely exasperated. 'Once and for all, Ruth,' he announced, standing and facing her, 'I would like you to understand that what happened last night was nothing whatever to do with alcohol. You've very adroitly rationalised the whole affair to your own satisfaction, but your deductions are based on complete fallacy.'

He paused, and then went on, choosing his words with obvious care. 'I am willing to grant you that it was an aberration, some sort of odd psychic delusion brought on by suggestion or hypnosis or whatever, but I was stone cold sober from first to last, and extremely upset into the bargain.'

Ruth looked indignant. '*You* were upset indeed! What about me?' she wanted to know.

'You behaved with a stolid, obtuse lack of comprehension that frankly shocked me,' Charles told her angrily.

Ruth took a breath. 'I consider that I was remarkably patient,' she insisted. 'I shall know better next time.'

'Instead of putting out a gently comradely hand to guide me, you shouted staccato orders at me like a ghastly sergeant major,' Charles complained.

'You seem to forget,' Ruth pointed out, 'that you gratuitously insulted me.'

'I did not,' he replied indignantly.

'You called me a guttersnipe,' Ruth reminded him. 'You told me to shut up – and when I quietly suggested that we should go up to bed, you said, with the most disgusting leer, that it was an immoral suggestion.'

'I was talking to Elvira!' Charles shouted in exasperation.

'If you were,' replied Ruth with an expression that came close to a sneer, 'I can only say that it conjures up a fragrant picture of your first marriage.'

Charles looked affronted. 'My first marriage was perfectly charming,' he replied in his most dignified manner, 'and I think it's in the worst possible taste for you to sneer at it.'

'I am not nearly so interested in your first marriage as you think I am,' Ruth told him. 'It's your second marriage that is absorbing me at the moment. It seems to me to be on the rocks.'

'Only because you persist in taking up this ridiculous attitude,' Charles exclaimed.

'My attitude,' Ruth virtually shouted, 'is that of any normal woman whose husband gets drunk and hurls abuse at her.'

'I was not drunk!' Charles shouted back at her, and strode across to the mantelpiece.

'Be quiet, or they'll hear you in the kitchen,' Ruth warned him.

'I don't care if they hear me in the Folkstone town hall,' Charles retorted, still at shouting level. 'I – was – not – drunk!'

'Control yourself, Charles,' Ruth snapped at him.

'How can I control myself in the face of your idiotic damned stubbornness?' he asked angrily, though not quite as loudly as before. 'It's positively giving me claustrophobia.'

'Then you'd better ring up Dr Bradman,' Ruth suggested unsympathetically.

At this moment, Edith came into the room with a tray to clear away the breakfast things. 'Can I clear, please, ma'am?' she asked Ruth.

'Yes, Edith,' replied Ruth, going across to the window.

'Cook wants to know about lunch, ma'am,' Edith informed her.

Ruth looked at her husband. 'Will you be in to lunch, Charles?' she asked coldly.

'Please don't worry about me,' he replied in the same tone. 'I shall be perfectly happy with a bottle of gin in my bedroom.'

'Don't be silly, dear,' Ruth told him, attempting to sound pleasant for the sake of the maid, to whom she said, 'Tell cook we shall both be in, Edith.'

'Yes'm,' was Edith's reply.

'Just wait a second,' Ruth called to the maid as she was about to leave the room with the breakfast tray she had loaded. Then, conversationally, Ruth said to Charles, 'I'm going into Hythe this morning. Is there anything you want?'

'Yes, a great deal,' Charles replied emphatically, 'but I doubt if you could get it in Hythe.'

Ruth turned to the maid, 'Tell cook to put Alka-Seltzer down on my list please, Edith,' she ordered.

'Yes'm,' was, of course, Edith's reply, as she waited for any further instructions.

Ruth was now looking out of the window. After a pause, she observed, 'It's clouding over.'

'You have a genius for understatement,' Charles commented sarcastically.

'Don't worry about the table, Edith. I'll put it away,' Ruth told Edith, dismissing her with a gesture, at which the maid uttered a final 'Yes'm' and, breathing heavily, staggered out of the room at a brisk pace, carrying the tray.

Ruth began to fold the cloth from the breakfast table, and Charles came over to her.

'Please, Ruth,' he implored, 'be reasonable.'

'I'm perfectly reasonable,' she responded, continuing to fuss about at the breakfast table, moving the chairs away.

'I wasn't pretending,' Charles continued, persuasively. 'I really did believe that I saw Elvira, and when I heard her voice I was appalled.'

'You put up with it for five years,' Ruth observed unsympathetically, as she finished putting the chairs against the wall.

Charles moved the breakfast table away from the centre of the room. 'When I saw her,' he continued, 'I had the shock of my life. That's why I dropped the glass.'

'But you *couldn't* have seen her,' Ruth pointed out.

'I know I couldn't have, but I did,' he insisted.

Ruth looked at him steadily for a moment. 'All right,' she said, 'I'm willing to concede that you imagined you did.'

Charles gave a sigh of relief. 'That's what I've been trying to explain to you for hours,' he exclaimed.

'Well then, there's obviously something wrong with you,' Ruth observed.

'Exactly,' he replied, going over to sit on an arm of the sofa. 'There *is* something wrong with me – something fundamentally wrong with me. That's why I've been imploring your sympathy, and all I got was a sterile temperance lecture.'

Ruth frowned. 'You *had* been drinking, Charles – there's no denying that,' she pointed out.

'No more than usual,' he insisted.

'Well, how do you account for it, then?' she wanted to know.

Charles suddenly became frantic again. 'I can't account for it,' he yelled at her. 'That's what's so absolutely awful.'

Ruth thought for a moment, and then, adopting a practical tone, she asked, 'Did you feel quite well yesterday? During the day, I mean.'

'Yes, of course I did,' he replied.

'What did you have for lunch?'

'I can't remember,' Charles told her. 'But you ought to know,' he added, 'You had lunch with me.'

Ruth thought. 'Let me see now,' she murmured. 'There was a delicious lemon sole, and that cheese thing, and –'

'Why should having a cheese thing for lunch make me

see my deceased wife after dinner?' Charles asked querulously. 'That doesn't make any sense.'

'You never know,' Ruth contradicted him. 'It was rather
rich, that cheese dish.'

'Well, why didn't you see your dead husband then?'
Charles asked her, holding out his arms in a gesture of
helplessness. 'You ate just as much of the cheese thing as I
did.'

Ruth shook her head. 'This is not getting us anywhere at
all,' she observed.

'Of course it isn't,' Charles agreed. 'And it won't get us
anywhere as long as you insist on ascribing supernatural
phenomena to colonic irritation.'

'Supernatural grandmother!' Ruth snapped.

'I admit she'd have been much less agitating,' Charles
muttered to himself.

Standing behind an armchair, Ruth looked at him
steadily for a moment, before suggesting, 'Perhaps you
ought to see a nerve specialist. You know, a psychiatrist or
someone like that.'

'I am not in the least neurotic,' Charles insisted, 'and I
never have been.'

She tried again. 'Why not ask Dr Bradman if he can
recommend a psychoanalyst?'

Charles shook his head irritably. 'I refuse to endure
months of expensive humiliation,' he replied, 'only to be

told at the end of it that at the age of four I was in love with my rocking horse.'

Ruth held out her hands in a gesture of helplessness. 'What do you suggest, then?' she asked him.

'I don't suggest anything,' Charles replied. 'I can't think what to do. I'm just profoundly uneasy.'

Ruth sat in the armchair. 'Perhaps there's something pressing on your brain,' she wondered aloud.

Charles gave another dismissive shake of the head. 'If there were something pressing on my brain,' he declared, 'I should have violent headaches, shouldn't I?'

'Not necessarily,' said Ruth. 'An uncle of mine had a lump the size of a cricket ball pressing on his brain for years, and he never felt a thing.'

'I'm sure I would know if I had anything like that,' Charles answered, getting up from the sofa and going over to the fireplace.

'My uncle didn't know,' Ruth pointed out.

'Well, what happened to him?' Charles asked her.

'He had the lump taken out, and he's been as bright as a button ever since,' Ruth replied.

'Did he have delusions of any sort?' Charles wanted to know. 'Did he think he saw things that weren't there? Some dead ancestor or anything?'

'No, I don't think so,' Ruth admitted after some thought.

'Well, what the hell are we talking about him for,

BLITHE SPIRIT

then?' Charles asked irritably. 'It's a sheer waste of valuable time.'

'I only brought him up as an example,' Ruth protested.

Charles groaned. 'I really do think I'm going mad.'

Ruth looked at him anxiously. 'How do you feel right now?' she asked.

He looked puzzled. 'Physically, do you mean?'

'No, I mean altogether,' she explained.

After due reflection Charles replied, 'Apart from being extremely worried, I feel quite normal.'

'Good,' said Ruth. 'You're not hearing or seeing anything in the least unusual?'

Charles shook his head. 'Not a thing,' he told her.

At that moment, the grey apparition of Elvira glided in through the French windows, carrying a bunch of roses. She crossed to the writing table, threw into a wastepaper basket the zinnias that were in the vase on the table, and put her roses into the vase. The roses were as grey as the rest of her.

'You've absolutely ruined that border by the sundial,' Elvira's apparition said, addressing Charles. 'It's awful now. It looks just like a mixed salad.'

109

Chapter Eight

—▬—

Charles heard clearly what Elvira's apparition had said, although Ruth heard nothing at all. When he turned and saw Elvira standing by the writing table, he was appalled. 'Oh, my God!' he shouted.

'What's the matter now?' Ruth asked him, sounding impatient.

'She's here again,' Charles gasped, looking in dismay at Elvira.

'What do you mean?' Ruth said irritably. 'Who's here again?'

'Elvira,' Charles replied, still staring at the apparition.

'Charles, pull yourself together and don't be absurd,' Ruth ordered him.

Elvira spoke again, still criticising the garden. 'It's all

those nasturtiums – they're so vulgar,' she exclaimed.

'I like nasturtiums,' Charles told her, in an irritable tone of voice.

'You like what?' Ruth asked him, perplexed.

Arranging her grey roses in the vase, Elvira continued, 'They're all right in moderation, but not a whole mass of them like that. They look quite beastly.'

Charles went over to his wife. 'Help me, Ruth,' he begged her. 'You've got to help me.'

Ruth retreated from him. 'What did you mean about nasturtiums?' she asked.

Charles came close to her and took her hands. 'Never mind about that now,' he said hastily. 'I tell you she's here again.'

Elvira strolled over to the sofa. 'You two have been having a nice old scene, haven't you?' she observed, grinning maliciously. 'I could hear you from right down at the other end of the garden.'

'Please mind your own business,' Charles snapped at her.

Believing this remark was meant for her, Ruth exploded in fury. 'If you behaving like a lunatic isn't my business, I don't know what is,' she screamed at him.

Elvira giggled. 'I expect your row was about me, wasn't it?' she said to Charles. 'I know I ought to feel sorry, but I'm not. I'm delighted.'

'How can you be so inconsiderate?' Charles asked in exasperation.

Ruth exploded with rage. 'Inconsiderate!' she cried shrilly. 'I like that, I must say.'

'Ruth – darling – please,' Charles began, but Ruth interrupted him angrily. 'I've done everything I can to help you,' she told him. 'I've controlled myself admirably – and I should like to say here and now that I don't believe a word about your damned hallucination. You're up to something, Charles Condomine. There's been a certain furtiveness in your manner for weeks. Why can't you simply be honest and tell me what it is?'

'You're wrong,' Charles attempted to assure her. 'You're completely wrong. I haven't been in the least furtive. I –'

'You're trying to upset me,' Ruth cried. She broke away from him. 'For some obscure reason, you're trying to goad me into doing something that I might regret. Well, I won't stand for it any more. You're making me utterly miserable.'

She fell into the sofa and burst into tears.

Charles came over to her. 'Ruth – please,' he pleaded, but she pushed him away. 'Don't come near me,' she sobbed.

'Oh, let her have a nice cry,' Elvira called to Charles, as she sauntered around the room. 'It'll do her good.'

'You're utterly heartless!' Charles screamed at Elvira, but it was Ruth who responded with a shocked 'Me? Heartless?'

'I was not talking to you,' Charles shouted wildly to his wife. 'I was talking to Elvira.'

'Go on talking to her then,' Ruth cried. 'Talk to her until you're blue in the face, but just don't talk to me.'

Charles went over to the apparition of his dead first wife. 'Help me, Elvira,' he pleaded.

'How?' Elvira asked, nonchalantly.

'I don't know,' he exclaimed in exasperation. 'Make her see you, or something.'

'I'm afraid I couldn't manage that,' Elvira replied. 'It's technically the most difficult business. It's really frightfully complicated, you know. It takes years of study –' She shook her head and gave him a sad smile.

Charles stared at Elvira intently. 'You are really here, aren't you?' he asked her. 'I mean, you're not just an illusion?'

'I may be an illusion,' she told him, 'but I'm most definitely here.'

'Can you tell me how you got here?' he asked.

'I told you last night,' Elvira reminded him. 'It seems you asked for me, but I don't exactly know how I got here.'

'Well, I certainly didn't ask for you,' Charles insisted, 'but since you're here now, you must make me a promise that, in future, you will only come and talk to me when I'm alone.'

Elvira pouted. 'How unkind you are, Charles – making me feel so unwanted,' she complained. 'I've never been treated so rudely.'

'I don't mean to be rude to you, Elvira,' Charles hastened to assure her, 'but you must surely see –'

'It's all your fault,' she interrupted him. 'It's your own fault for having married a woman who is incapable of seeing beyond the nose on her face. If she had a grain of real sympathy or affection for you, she'd believe what you tell her.'

'That's nonsense,' Charles expostulated. 'How could you expect anybody to believe this?'

'You'd be surprised how gullible people are,' Elvira told him, chuckling. 'We often laugh about it on the other side.'

Ruth had by now stopped crying, and was staring at Charles in horror. Suddenly she got up, went over to him, and placed a hand tenderly on his arm. 'Charles,' she said gently.

'Yes, dear?' he responded, surprised and relieved by her tone.

'I'm awfully sorry I was cross,' she told him.

'But, my dear –' he began.

He was not allowed to continue. 'I understand everything now,' Ruth assured him. 'I do, really.'

'You do?' he asked in astonishment.

'Of course I do,' said Ruth, patting his arm reassuringly.

'Look out,' Elvira warned. 'I'll bet you she's up to something.'

'Will you please be quiet!' Charles snapped at Elvira.

The reply, however, came from Ruth. 'Of course, darling,' she murmured soothingly. 'We'll all be quiet, won't we? We'll be as quiet as little mice.'

Charles groaned. 'Ruth darling, listen – ,' he began, but she continued to speak soothingly to him. 'I want you to come upstairs with me and go to bed,' she told him.

Elvira sniggered. 'The way that woman keeps going on about bed is nothing short of disgusting,' she commented bitchily.

'I'll deal with you later,' Charles warned Elvira, to which Ruth replied, 'Very well, darling. You'll deal with me later. But come along now.'

Ruth tried to drag him out of the room, but Charles resisted her. 'What are you up to?' he asked querulously.

'I'm not up to anything,' Ruth assured him. 'I just want you to go quietly to bed, and wait there until Doctor Bradman comes –'

'No, Ruth – you're wrong,' Charles insisted, trying to free himself from her grasp.

'Come, dear,' Ruth insisted firmly.

Elvira chuckled. 'She'll have you in a straitjacket before you know where you are,' she warned Charles facetiously.

He broke free from Ruth, and came over to Elvira. 'Help me – you must help me,' he cried frantically.

'My dear,' Elvira replied, obviously enjoying herself, 'I

would help you with the greatest pleasure, of course, but I simply can't think how.'

Charles was struck by a sudden idea. 'I know how!' he cried.

He went back to Ruth. 'Listen, Ruth –'

'Yes, dear,' she enquired sweetly, taking hold of his arm again.

'If I promise to go to bed,' said Charles, 'will you let me stay here for five minutes longer? And you must stay here with me.'

Ruth looked dubious. 'I really think it would be better –' she began, only to be interrupted by Charles, who begged her urgently, 'Bear with me, please, darling. However mad it may seem to you. Bear with me for just five minutes longer.'

Ruth let go of him. 'Very well. What is it?' she asked, attempting to sound patient.

'Sit down,' Charles ordered her.

She obeyed. 'All right – there,' she said as she settled herself on the sofa.

He stood before her, holding his arm up for attention. 'Now listen,' he began. 'Listen carefully.'

'Have a cigarette, Charles,' Elvira interjected. 'It will help to soothe your nerves.'

'I don't want a cigarette,' he replied shortly.

'Then you shan't have one, darling,' Ruth assured him in her most indulgent manner.

Charles ploughed on. 'Ruth,' he began, looking earnestly and steadily at her as she sat gazing more than somewhat anxiously at him. 'I want to explain to you clearly and without emotion that, beyond any shadow of doubt, the ghost or shade, or whatever you like to call it, of my first wife Elvira, is in this room now.'

'Yes, dear,' Ruth replied soothingly.

'I know you don't believe it,' Charles continued, 'and you're trying valiantly to humour me, but I intend to prove it to you.'

Ruth smiled up at him reassuringly. 'Why not lie down and have a nice rest, and you can prove anything you want to, later on,' she suggested.

'Elvira might not be here later on,' Charles pointed out, at which Elvira called playfully to him, 'Don't worry – she will.'

'Oh God!' Charles groaned.

'Hush, dear,' Ruth murmured in an attempt to calm him, but he had already turned away from her, and was addressing Elvira. 'Now, Elvira, you must promise you'll do what I ask,' he ordered her.

'That all depends on what it is,' Elvira replied.

Charles took his position halfway between them both. 'Ruth,' he said to his wife, 'do you see that bowl of flowers on the piano?'

'Yes, dear,' she replied. 'I arranged them myself this morning.'

'Very untidily, if I may say so,' Elvira interjected.

'You may not,' Charles snapped, at which Ruth then said, in submissive tones, 'Very well, darling – I never will again. I promise.'

Charles ignored this. 'Elvira will now carry that bowl of flowers to the mantelpiece and back again,' he announced. Turning to Elvira, he added, 'You will, Elvira, won't you? Just to please me?'

'I don't really see why I should,' Elvira replied. 'You've been quite insufferable to me ever since I materialised.'

'Please, Elvira,' he pleaded.

'Oh, all right, I will – just this once,' Elvira promised. 'Not that I approve of all these weird carryings on.'

She went over to the piano, and Charles addressed his wife. 'Now, Ruth – watch carefully,' he instructed her.

'Very well, dear,' Ruth replied, patiently.

'Go on, Elvira,' Charles instructed his former wife. 'Take the flowers to the mantelpiece and back again.'

Elvira sighed, took a bowl of pansies from the piano, carried it slowly across the room, and then suddenly pushed it towards Ruth's face.

Ruth jumped to her feet. 'How dare you, Charles!' she shouted in a fury. 'You ought to be ashamed of yourself.'

'What on earth for?' Charles asked her, perplexed.

'It's a trick,' Ruth screamed hysterically. 'I know perfectly well it has to be a trick. You've been working up to this. It's all part of some horrible plan –'

'It isn't – I swear it isn't,' Charles insisted. He turned to his first wife. 'Elvira – do something else, for God's sake,' he implored her.

'Certainly,' Elvira chortled. 'Anything to oblige, darling.'

Ruth was becoming really frightened. 'You want to get rid of me,' she screamed at Charles. 'You're trying to drive me out of my mind.'

'Don't be silly,' Charles retorted, but Ruth continued, 'You're cruel and sadistic, and I'll never forgive you.'

It was at this moment that Elvira picked up a chair, and waltzed about the room with it before placing it against the wall.

'I'm not going to put up with this any longer,' Ruth shouted, terrified of objects apparently able to move around without aid. She began to run from the room, but Charles grabbed her. 'You must believe it – you must,' he implored her.

'Let me go immediately,' Ruth insisted, trying to get away from him.

'That was Elvira running around with the chair – it really was,' Charles attempted to convince Ruth. 'I swear it was.'

Ruth went on struggling to free herself from his grasp. 'Let me go,' she cried again.

'Ruth, please –' he began, as Ruth broke free of him and

ran to the French windows. Elvira, however, got there ahead of her and shut the windows in her face.

Ruth turned, looking at her husband with eyes of horror. 'Charles, this is madness,' she gasped. 'Sheer madness. It's some sort of auto-suggestion, isn't it? Some form of hypnotism? Swear to me it's only that.'

She rushed to Charles and clung to him. 'Swear to me it's only that,' she repeated urgently.

Elvira took an expensive vase from the mantelpiece and crashed it into the grate, crying 'Hypnotism, my foot!', at which Ruth gave a scream and collapsed in a state of violent hysteria.

Chapter Nine

—▬—

At about half past four on the following afternoon, the sitting room showed no signs of the previous evening's chaos. Ruth sat alone at the tea table, which was set in front of the fireplace. She was now perfectly calm after a night of exhausted sleep – alone, for she had banished Charles to another room – and she had spent the morning avoiding her husband, and making plans to deal with the impossible, indeed unbelievable, situation.

After a moment or two, Ruth got up and, frowning thoughtfully, went over to the mantelpiece to take a cigarette from a box. As she returned to the tea table, the front-door bell rang. Ruth straightened herself up as though preparing for a difficult interview, and took a deep breath. When Edith entered the room to announce, 'Madame

Arcati has called to see you, ma'am,' the medium came in, and Edith then left immediately.

Madame Arcati was wearing a tweed coat and skirt, a great many amber beads, and a beret perched on top of her head. 'My dear Mrs Condomine,' she greeted Ruth, 'I came directly I got your message.'

'That was very kind of you,' Ruth replied politely.

'Kind?' Madame Arcati exclaimed briskly. 'Nonsense! Nothing kind about it. I look upon it as an outing.'

'I'm so glad,' Ruth responded, smiling briefly. She gestured to the teapot and cups on the table. 'Will you have some tea?' she asked.

'China or Indian?' the medium enquired, sounding anxious.

'It's China tea,' Ruth told her.

Madame Arcati nodded her head in satisfaction. 'Good!' she exclaimed. 'I never touch Indian. It upsets my vibrations.'

Ruth made no comment on this. Gesturing to a chair, she invited the medium to sit, and she herself poured tea for them both.

Madame Arcati kept turning her head and sniffing. 'I find this room very interesting,' she said with fervour. 'Very interesting indeed. I noticed as much the other night.'

'I'm not entirely surprised,' Ruth murmured dryly.

Sitting down after pulling off her cape and gloves,

Madame Arcati asked, 'Have you ever been to Cowden Manor, Mrs Condomine?'

Ruth looked blank. 'No, I'm afraid I haven't,' she replied.

'That's a very interesting place too,' Madame Arcati informed her. 'It strikes you like a blow between the eyes, the moment you walk into the drawing room.' Without a pause, she went on, 'I'll take two lumps of sugar, please, and no milk at all.'

Ruth put sugar into the medium's cup and handed it to her, saying as she did so, 'I am profoundly disturbed, Madame Arcati, and I desperately need your help.'

'Aha! I thought as much,' Madame Arcati replied, adding without a pause, 'What's in those dainty little sandwiches?'

'Cucumber,' Ruth told her, trying not to sound impatient.

The medium took a sandwich from the plate. 'Cucumber. Couldn't be better,' she exclaimed. 'Now, fire away, Mrs Condomine.'

Ruth hesitated for a moment. 'It's most awfully difficult to explain,' she began, only to be interrupted immediately. 'Facts first, explanations afterwards,' the medium instructed her, speaking as clearly as she could with a mouth full of bread and cucumber.

'It's the facts that are so difficult to explain,' Ruth told her. 'They're so fantastic.'

Madame Arcati nodded vigorously in agreement with

Ruth. 'Facts very often are,' she observed. 'Take creative talent, for instance. How do you account for that? Look at Shakespeare and Michelangelo! Try to explain Mozart snatching sounds out of the air and putting them down on paper when he was practically still a baby. Facts! Plain facts!'

She munched on her sandwich, and continued, 'I know it's the fashion nowadays to ascribe absolutely everything to glands, but my reply to that is fiddle-de-dee!'

Ruth looked perplexed. 'Yes, I'm sure you're quite right,' she agreed helplessly.

Madame Arcati wagged a finger at her. 'There are more things in heaven and earth than are dreamt of in your philosophy, Mrs Condomine,' she intoned portentously.

'There certainly are,' Ruth agreed again, this time with great fervour.

Madame Arcati looked at her expectantly. 'Come now, take the plunge – out with it, whatever it is,' she ordered.

Ruth was about to reply when the medium continued, 'I know – you've heard strange noises in the night, no doubt. Boards creaking, doors slamming, subdued moaning in the corridors. Is that it?'

'No, I'm afraid it isn't. If only it were,' Ruth replied.

Madame Arcati looked anxious. 'No sudden gusts of cold wind, I hope?' she asked, taking another sandwich as she spoke.

'No, it's much, much worse than that,' Ruth told her.

About to put the sandwich in her mouth, Madame Arcati changed her mind. Placing the sandwich back on the plate, she declared, 'Go on, I'm all attention.'

Ruth made an effort to speak calmly. 'I know it sounds idiotic,' she admitted, 'but the other night – during the seance – something very strange happened –'

'I knew it!' Madame Arcati interrupted gleefully. 'It was probably a poltergeist. They're enormously cunning, you know. They sometimes lie low for days on end, and then –'

In no mood to be informed about the habits of poltergeists, Ruth interrupted her urgently. 'You know that my husband had been married before, don't you?' she asked Madame Arcati.

'Yes – I have heard it mentioned,' the medium replied, nodding her head.

Ruth continued. 'His first wife, Elvira, died comparatively young –'

'Where?' Madame Arcati asked immediately and with sharpness in her tone.

'Here – in this house,' Ruth told her. 'Actually, in this very room.'

Madame Arcati gave a shrill whistle. 'Whew! I'm beginning to see daylight!' she exclaimed with enthusiasm.

Ruth went on. 'She was convalescing after pneumonia, and one evening, listening to the radio in here, she started to laugh helplessly at one of the BBC's musical programmes, and she died of a sudden heart attack.'

Madame Arcati nodded her head thoughtfully. 'And I assume she materialised the other evening. Was it after I had gone?' she enquired.

'She materialised, but not to me,' Ruth explained. 'She apparently materialised to my husband.'

Madame Arcati got to her feet. 'Capital!' she exclaimed impulsively. 'Capital!' She clasped her hands in glee. 'Oh, but that's splendid,' she shouted.

Ruth looked affronted. 'From your own professional standpoint,' she told the medium coldly, 'I can see that it might be regarded as a major achievement, but I must say that I –'

Oblivious to Ruth's feelings, Madame Arcati interrupted to express her own great delight. 'A magnificent triumph, my dear!' she exclaimed happily. 'Nothing more nor less than a magnificent triumph!'

Ruth continued to express her own train of thought. 'I must say,' she repeated, 'that from my own personal point of view it is, to say the least of it, highly embarrassing.'

Now walking excitedly about the room, Madame Arcati continued to shout joyfully, 'At last! At last! A genuine materialisation.'

'Please sit down again, Madame Arcati,' Ruth urged her, but the medium continued to pace about the room excitedly. 'How could anyone sit down at a moment like this?' she exclaimed. 'It's tremendous! I haven't had such a success since the Sudbury case, when I conjured up –'

Ruth's voice was extremely sharp as she interrupted. 'I must insist upon you sitting down and controlling your natural exuberance,' she told the medium. 'I appreciate fully your immense pride in your achievement, but I would like to point out that it has made my position in this house untenable, and that I hold you entirely responsible for this.'

Madame Arcati abruptly ceased her perambulations, and went over to sit in the armchair, looking extremely contrite. 'Please forgive me, Mrs Condomine,' she said most apologetically. 'I am being abominably selfish. I do apologise. Tell me, how can I help you?'

Ruth's immediate and vigorous response to this was, 'How can you help me? How? By sending this wretched woman back immediately to where she came from, of course.'

Madame Arcati looked grave. 'I'm afraid that is more easily said than done,' she murmured, shaking her head sadly.

'Do you mean to tell me,' Ruth asked, 'that she is liable to stay here indefinitely?'

'Well, it's very difficult to say,' Madame Arcati admitted. 'I fear it largely depends on her, and on what she wants.'

'But my dear Madame Arcati –' Ruth began. However, she was interrupted by the medium, who asked somewhat excitedly, 'Where is she now?'

Ruth sighed. 'My husband has driven her into Folkestone. Apparently she was anxious to see an old friend of hers who is staying at the Grand Hotel there.'

Madame Arcati took a notebook from her handbag, and very quickly wrote in it. Then she looked up at Ruth.

'Forgive this formality, Mrs Condomine,' she exclaimed excitedly, 'but I shall have to make a report to the Psychical Research people.'

'Well, if you must, you must,' Ruth replied. 'But,' she added firmly, 'I would be very much obliged if there were no names mentioned.'

The medium nodded gravely. 'The report will be extremely confidential, I assure you,' she said in an exaggerated whisper.

'After all, this is a small village, you know,' Ruth pointed out. 'And any gossip would be most undesirable.'

'I quite understand,' Madame Arcati assured Ruth. After a vigorous nod of the head, she continued, 'Now, did you say that she is visible only to your husband?'

'Yes,' Ruth replied bluntly.

Madame Arcati made a note in her book. 'Visible only to husband,' she murmured as she wrote. She then looked up at Ruth and asked, 'Audible too, I presume?'

'Extremely audible,' was Ruth's dry response to this.

'Extremely audible,' Madame Arcati repeated as she noted this down before asking, 'And was your husband greatly devoted to her?'

It was with a slight irritation creeping into her voice that Ruth replied, 'Yes, I believe so.'

'Husband extremely devoted,' the medium murmured as she scribbled this down, her face screwed up in intense excitement.

Feeling, or perhaps hoping, that 'extremely devoted' might be an overstatement of the case, Ruth said, 'Well, it was apparently a reasonably happy marriage.'

'Oh, tut tut!' the medium responded.

'I beg your pardon?' Ruth asked, sounding somewhat annoyed.

Madame Arcati chose to ignore Ruth's reaction, and asked her, 'Can you tell me exactly when she passed over?'

'Seven years ago,' was Ruth's terse reply to this.

'Aha!' Madame Arcati exclaimed. 'That means she must have been on the waiting list.'

Ruth looked perplexed. 'The waiting list?' she queried.

'Yes,' the medium replied. 'Otherwise, you see, she would have gone beyond the materialisation stage by now.' She thought for a moment, chewing the end of her pencil, and then continued. 'She must have marked herself down for a return visit, and she'd never have been able to manage it unless there were a very strong influence at work.'

'Do you mean,' Ruth asked her incredulously, 'that Charles – my husband – wanted her back all that much?'

Madame Arcati nodded her head vigorously. 'Quite

possible,' she replied. 'Or, of course, it might have been her own determination.'

'That sounds much more likely,' Ruth observed hopefully.

Madame Arcati pursed her lips and looked thoughtful. 'Would you say that the first Mrs Condomine was a strong character?' she asked.

It was with rising annoyance that Ruth replied, 'I really don't know, Madame Arcati. After all, I never met her. Nor am I particularly interested in how and why she got here. I am solely concerned with the question of how to get her away from here again as soon as possible.'

'I fully sympathise with you, Mrs Condomine,' the medium replied, again with a vigorous nod of the head. 'And I assure you that I will do anything in my power to help. But at the moment, I fear I cannot offer any great hopes.'

'But I always thought that there was a way of exorcising ghosts – some sort of ritual,' Ruth exclaimed, now looking thoroughly exasperated.

'Do you mean the old "bell, book and candle" method?' Madame Arcati asked her.

'Well, yes,' Ruth replied. 'I suppose I do.'

Madame Arcati shook her head. 'I'm afraid that's poppycock, Mrs Condomine,' she declared. 'Oh, I admit it was quite effective in the old days of genuine religious belief, but that's all changed now.' She looked very grave as she continued, 'I understand that the decline of faith has been causing grave concern in the spirit world.'

'Has it indeed?' Ruth snorted impatiently.

'Yes, I fear so,' Madame Arcati replied. 'There was a time, of course, when a drop of holy water could send even a poltergeist scampering for cover. But not any more.' Shaking her head with great sadness, she declaimed, 'Où sont les neiges d'Antan?'

With a look of absolute determination, Ruth addressed the medium. 'Be that as it may, Madame Arcati,' she said firmly, 'I must beg of you to do your utmost to dematerialise my husband's first wife as soon as possible.'

The medium gave a sigh. 'The time has come for me to admit to you frankly, Mrs Condomine,' she confessed, 'that I haven't the faintest idea of how to set about it.'

Ruth rose from her seat with vigour. 'Do you mean to sit there and tell me,' she exclaimed, her voice rising almost to a shout, 'that, having mischievously conjured up this ghost or spirit or whatever she is, and placed me in a hideous position, you are unable to do anything about it at all?'

'Honesty is the best policy,' Madame Arcati replied primly.

'But that's absolutely outrageous!' Ruth expostulated, striding across to the fireplace. 'I ought to hand you over to the police.'

'You go too far, Mrs Condomine,' Madame Arcati retorted in high indignation.

'I go too far, indeed,' Ruth shouted in a fury. 'Do you realise what your insane amateur meddling has done?'

The medium drew herself up to her not very great height, and announced with icy dignity, 'I have been a professional since I was a child, Mrs Condomine. "Amateur" is a word I cannot tolerate.'

Ruth's retort to this was, 'It seems to me to be the height of amateurishness to evoke malignant spirits and not be able to get rid of them again.'

Madame Arcati retained her dignity. 'I was in a trance,' she explained coldly. 'Anything might happen when I am in a trance.'

Ruth glared at her unsympathetically. 'Well, all I can suggest,' she told the medium, 'is that you go into another one immediately, and get this damned woman out of my house.'

'I can't go into trances at a moment's notice,' Madame Arcati explained patiently. 'It takes hours of preparation, in addition to which I have to be extremely careful of my diet for days beforehand.'

Ruth was about to comment on this, but the medium forestalled her by continuing, 'Today, for instance, I happened to have lunch with friends, and I had pigeon pie which – with those delicious cucumber sandwiches of yours on top of it – would make a trance at this moment out of the question.'

A pregnant silence ensued momentarily, broken by Ruth exclaiming, 'Well, you'll jolly well have to do *something*.'

Madame Arcati nodded her head in affirmation. 'Indeed, yes. I shall report the whole matter to the Society for Psychical Research at the earliest possible moment,' she promised.

'Do you expect they will be able to do anything?' Ruth asked her.

'I doubt it,' Madame Arcati admitted. 'They'd send an investigation committee, I expect, and do a lot of questioning and wall-tapping and mumbo jumbo, and then they'd have a conference, and you would probably have to go up to London to testify, and –'

'It's all too humiliating,' Ruth protested. 'It really is.' By now she was close to tears.

Madame Arcati rose from her seat, and went over to her. 'Please try not to upset yourself, Mrs Condomine,' she urged. 'Nothing at all can be achieved by upsetting yourself.'

'It's all very well for you to talk like that, Madame Arcati,' Ruth replied, 'but you don't seem to have the faintest realisation of how upsetting my position is.'

'You must try to look on the bright side,' the medium urged with an encouraging smile.

'Bright side indeed!' Ruth snapped. 'If your husband's first wife suddenly appeared from the grave and came to live in the house with you, do you suppose you'd be able to look on the bright side? Tell me that!'

'I resent your tone, Mrs Condomine,' Madame Arcati told her firmly. 'I really do.'

'You most decidedly have no right to,' Ruth snapped. 'You are entirely to blame for the whole horrible situation.'

'Kindly remember that I came here the other night on your own invitation,' the medium reminded her, wagging a finger in Ruth's face.

'No, you did not. It was on my husband's invitation,' Ruth corrected her.

The medium ignored this. 'I did what I was requested to do,' she pointed out to Ruth. 'And that was to give a seance and establish contact with the other side. I had no idea that there was any ulterior motive mixed up with it.'

Ruth looked puzzled at this. 'Ulterior motive?' she queried

'Your husband was obviously eager to get in touch with his former wife,' Madame Arcati explained. 'If I had been aware of that at the time, I should naturally have consulted you beforehand. After all, noblesse oblige!'

'I tell you he had no intention of trying to get in touch with anyone,' Ruth insisted. 'The whole thing was planned in order for him to gather material for a mystery story he is writing about a homicidal medium.'

Madame Arcati drew herself up with dignity. 'Am I to understand,' she asked icily, 'that I was invited only in a spirit of mockery? Is that what the seance was for?'

'No, not at all,' Ruth replied. 'He merely wanted to make notes of some of the tricks of the trade.'

Madame Arcati was, not surprisingly, incensed at this. 'Tricks of the trade!' she exploded in rage and indignation. 'This is insufferable! I've never been so insulted in my life. I feel that we have nothing more to say to one another, Mrs Condomine. Goodbye.' She turned to go.

'Please don't leave, Madame Arcati,' Ruth pleaded. 'Please –'

The medium turned back to face her. 'Your attitude from the outset has been most deeply unpleasant, Mrs Condomine,' she told Ruth. 'Some of your remarks have been discourteous in the extreme, and I should like to say, without umbrage, that if you and your husband were foolish enough to start tampering with the unseen for paltry motives and in a spirit of ribaldry, then whatever has happened to you is your own fault and, to coin a phrase, as far as I am concerned you can stew in your own juice.'

She snatched her gloves and cape, and strode majestically from the room. Ruth stared after her in dismay, and muttered 'Damn – Damn – Damn!' stubbing out her cigarette in an ashtray as she did so.

Chapter Ten

—▬—

Ruth was still standing by the tea table and looking furious when, after a moment or two, Charles came into the room accompanied by Elvira.

'What on earth was Madame Arcati doing here?' Charles asked his second wife.

'She came to tea,' Ruth replied shortly.

Charles looked puzzled. 'Did you invite her?' he queried.

'Of course I did,' Ruth informed him.

'But you never told me you were going to do that,' Charles complained.

'You never told me you were going to ask Elvira to live with us,' Ruth countered.

'I didn't,' Charles insisted.

'Oh, yes, you did, darling,' Elvira contradicted him as

she sauntered over to the tea table. 'It was your sub-conscious helping you out.'

Charles ignored this. 'What was the old girl so cross about?' he asked Ruth. 'She practically cut me dead as she was leaving just then.'

Ruth regarded him steadily. 'Probably because I told her the truth,' she said.

When Charles looked as though he did not understand what she meant, Ruth expanded her answer. 'I told her the truth about why we invited her the other evening.'

'Darling, that was quite unnecessary and most unkind,' Charles rebuked his wife.

'Not at all,' Ruth replied. 'She needed taking down a bit. She was blowing herself out like a pouter pigeon.'

'But why, exactly, did you ask her to tea?' Charles wanted to know.

It was Elvira who answered his question. 'To get me exorcised, of course,' she said. Contemplating the sand-wiches on the tea table, she continued, 'Oh dear, I wish I were able to eat. I did love cucumber sandwiches so much.'

'Is that true, Ruth?' Charles asked his wife.

'Is what true?' Ruth replied.

'What Elvira said just now,' he explained.

Ruth looked exasperated. 'Charles, you know perfectly well I can't hear what Elvira says,' she reminded him.

'She said that you got Madame Arcati here to try to get her exorcised,' Charles told her. 'Is that true?'

Ruth looked slightly uncomfortable as she answered, 'Well, we did discuss the possibilities.'

Elvira went to sit in the armchair with her legs over one of the arms. 'Now there's a snake in the grass for you,' she commented bitchily.

Charles confronted his wife in anger. 'Ruth, you had no right to do such a thing without consulting me,' he told her.

'On the contrary, I have every right,' Ruth insisted. 'The situation is absolutely impossible, and you know it.'

Charles shook his head impatiently. 'If only you'd make an effort, and try to be a little more friendly to Elvira,' he exclaimed, 'we might all have quite a jolly time.'

Ruth glared at him. 'I have no wish to have a jolly time with Elvira,' she snapped.

'This wife of yours is certainly bad-tempered, isn't she?' Elvira commented. 'I can't think why on earth you married her.'

'Ruth is naturally a bit upset,' Charles explained to Elvira. 'We must make allowances for that.'

'I was never bad-tempered though, was I, darling?' Elvira asked him, coquettishly. 'Not even when you were beastly to me and –'

'I was never beastly to you, Elvira,' Charles interrupted her.

By now, Ruth was thoroughly exasperated. 'Just exactly where is Elvira at the moment?' she asked Charles, irritably.

'She's sitting in the chair by the table,' Charles told her.

Ruth addressed what seemed to her to be an empty chair. 'Now, look here, Elvira,' she began. 'I suppose I shall have to call you Elvira, shan't I? I can't very well go on saying Mrs Condomine all the time. It would sound too silly.'

'I don't see why,' Elvira replied.

'Did she say anything?' Ruth asked Charles.

'She said she'd like nothing better,' he answered tactfully rather than truthfully.

Elvira giggled. 'You really are sweet, Charles darling – I worship you,' she cried.

Still addressing the chair, Ruth said, 'Now I wish to be absolutely honest with you, Elvira –'

'Hold on to your hats, boys!' Elvira shouted, as Ruth, not hearing this, continued, 'I admit that I did ask Madame Arcati here with a view to getting you exorcised, and I think that if you were in my position you'd have done exactly the same thing – wouldn't you?'

'I suppose so, but I wouldn't have done it quite so obviously,' Elvira replied.

'What did she say?' Ruth asked Charles.

'Nothing,' Charles lied. 'She just nodded her head and smiled.'

'Thank you, Elvira,' said Ruth with a forced smile.

'That's generous of you. I really would so much rather that there were no misunderstandings between us.'

'That's very sensible of you, Ruth,' Charles congratulated his wife. 'I agree entirely.'

Ruth addressed Elvira's chair again. 'Before we go any further, I want to ask you a very frank question,' she announced. 'Tell me, why did you really come here? I don't see how you could have hoped to achieve anything by it, beyond the immediate joke of making Charles into a sort of astral bigamist.'

Elvira, safe in her invisibility to Ruth, smiled wickedly. 'I came,' she replied, 'simply because the power of Charles's love tugged and tugged and tugged at me.' She looked across at Charles with a wicked smile. 'Didn't it, my sweet?' she asked him.

'Tell me what she said, Charles,' Ruth asked her husband.

Charles thought it politic to paraphrase Elvira's words. 'She merely said that she came because she wanted to see me again,' he told Ruth.

'Well, she's done that now, hasn't she? Why doesn't she leave?' Ruth wanted to know.

Charles looked highly embarrassed. 'Now, Ruth darling, we can't be inhospitable, can we?' he replied.

'I have no wish to be inhospitable, Elvira,' Ruth said, continuing to address Elvira's chair, 'but I should just like to have some idea of how long you intend to stay?'

'I don't know – I really don't know,' Elvira answered her. Then, with a giggle, she added, 'Isn't it awful?'

When Charles translated this as 'She doesn't know,' Ruth raised her eyebrows. 'Surely that's a little inconsiderate, isn't it,' she commented.

'Didn't the old spiritualist have any constructive ideas about getting rid of me?' Elvira asked Charles, who passed the question on to his wife. 'What did Madame Arcati say about how to make Elvira leave?' he asked Ruth.

'She said she couldn't do a thing about it,' Ruth replied, looking grim.

'Hurray!' Elvira shouted happily. She rose from the chair and went to the window, a wide grin on her face.

Charles attempted to console his wife. 'Don't be upset, Ruth dear,' he said. 'We shall soon adjust ourselves, you know. And you must admit it's a unique experience, isn't it?' When Ruth remained silent, he continued, 'I can see no valid reason why we shouldn't get a great deal of fun out of it.'

'Fun!' Ruth exclaimed angrily. 'Charles, how can you be so stupid! You must be out of your mind!'

Charles smiled at this. 'Not at all,' he replied smugly. 'I thought at first that I was going out of my mind, but now I must say I'm beginning to enjoy myself.'

Ruth suddenly burst into tears. 'Oh, Charles – Charles –' she sobbed, while Elvira muttered, 'Oh dear, she's off again.'

Charles addressed his spirit visitor. 'You really must try not to be so callous, Elvira,' he admonished her. 'Try to see Ruth's point of view a little.'

Hearing his words, Ruth ceased crying. 'I suppose that woman said something insulting. Is that so?' she asked Charles.

'No, dear,' he replied mendaciously. 'She didn't do anything of the sort.'

Ruth addressed the armchair where she assumed Elvira was still sitting. 'Now look here, Elvira,' she began, only to be stopped by Charles, who informed her, 'I'm afraid Elvira's over by the window now.'

'Why the hell can't she stay in the same place?' Ruth snapped.

'Temper again,' Elvira chortled. 'My poor Charles, what a terrible life you must be leading.'

'Do shut up, darling,' Charles begged her. 'You'll only make everything worse.'

Ruth glared at him. 'Who was that "darling" addressed to ?' she demanded to know. 'Her or me?'

'Both of you,' Charles replied wearily.

Ruth got up and stamped her foot. 'This is intolerable!' she said.

'For heaven's sake, don't get into another state,' Charles pleaded, to which Ruth replied, in a fury, 'I've been doing my level best to control myself ever since yesterday morning, and I'm damned if I'm going to try any more. The strain is far too much.'

Waving a hand towards the windows where she assumed Elvira to be, Ruth continued, 'She has the advantage of being able to say whatever she pleases, without me being able to hear her, but she can hear me all right, can't she, without any modified interpreting on your part?'

'Modified interpreting?' Charles exclaimed. 'I don't know what you mean.'

'Oh, yes, you do,' Ruth insisted. 'You haven't once told me what she really said – you wouldn't dare. Judging from her photograph, she's the type who would use the most unpleasant language –'

'Ruth – you're not to talk like that,' Charles admonished his wife.

However, there was now no stopping Ruth. 'I've been making polite conversation all through dinner last night, and breakfast and lunch today – and it's been a nightmare,' she shouted. 'I am not going to do it any longer. I don't like Elvira any more than she likes me, and what's more, I'm certain that I never could have liked her, dead or alive.' Ruth stalked around the room, her voice becoming increasingly strident. 'If, since her untimely arrival here the other evening, she had shown the slightest sign of good manners, the slightest sign of breeding, I might have felt differently towards her, but all she has done is try to make mischief between us, and have private jokes with you against me.'

She came up close to Charles and addressed him a little more quietly, but no less determinedly. 'I am now going up to my room,' she informed him, 'and I shall have my dinner sent up on a tray. You and Elvira can have the house to yourselves, and joke and gossip with each other to your heart's content.'

She turned to go, but then came back to Charles. 'The first thing I am going to do in the morning,' she informed him, 'is to go up to London and talk to someone at the Psychical Research Society to find out what they can do to help. And if they fail me, I shall go straight to the Archbishop of Canterbury.'

She strode out of the room, and Charles made a movement to follow her. 'Ruth, darling –' he began, but Elvira called to him, 'Just let her go. She's sure to calm down later on.'

Charles shook his head. 'It's unlike Ruth to behave like this,' he told Elvira. 'She is generally so equable. So good-natured.'

'No, she isn't. Not really,' Elvira contradicted him. 'Her mouth gives her away. It's a very hard mouth, Charles.'

'Her mouth's got nothing to do with it,' Charles said angrily. 'And I resent you discussing Ruth as though she were a horse.'

Elvira gazed at him for a moment, before asking, 'Do you really love her?'

'Of course I do,' Charles replied unhesitatingly.

'As much as you used to love me?'

Charles looked uncomfortable. 'Don't be silly,' he replied. 'It's all entirely different.'

'I'm so glad to hear that,' Elvira murmured. 'Nothing could ever have been quite the same, could it?'

Charles regarded her quizzically. 'You always behaved very badly,' he pointed out.

'Oh, Charles!' she exclaimed indignantly.

'And I'm grieved to see,' he continued, 'that your sojourn in the other world hasn't improved you in the least.'

Elvira curled up at one end of the sofa. 'Go on, darling,' she encouraged him. 'I love it when you pretend to be cross with me.'

'I'm not pretending,' Charles insisted. He waved a hand dismissively at her. 'I'm going up to talk to Ruth,' he announced.

'Cowardy custard,' Elvira taunted him.

'Don't be idiotic,' Charles told her. 'I can't let her go just like that – I must be a little more nice and sympathetic to her.'

'I don't see why,' Elvira exclaimed. 'If she's so set on being disagreeable, I should just let her get on with it.'

Charles shook his head impatiently. 'This whole business

is very difficult for her,' he pointed out. 'We must try to be fair.'

Elvira now shook her head vigorously. 'I think she should learn to be more adaptable,' she insisted.

'She probably will in time,' Charles replied. 'But it's been a great shock. You must realise that.'

'Has it been a shock for you too, darling?' Elvira asked skittishly.

'Of course,' he answered. 'What did you expect?'

'Has it been a nice shock?' she persisted.

Charles regarded her seriously. 'What exactly do you want from me, Elvira?' he asked her.

'Want? I don't know what you mean,' she replied.

'I seem to remember,' Charles told her, wagging a finger in her face, 'that whenever you were overpoweringly demure it usually meant that you wanted something.'

'Oh, Charles, it's horrid of you to be so suspicious,' Elvira exclaimed, pouting. 'All I want is to be with you.'

'Well, you are with me,' he pointed out to her.

'I mean alone with you, darling,' she explained. 'If you go and pamper Ruth and smarm all over her, she'll probably come flouncing down again. And our lovely quiet evening together will be absolutely ruined.'

Charles smiled at Elvira. 'You're incorrigibly selfish,' he told her. 'You always were.'

'Well, I haven't seen you for seven years,' she reminded

him. 'It's only natural that I should want a little time alone with you. Just to talk over old times.'

She paused, and then continued, 'Well, I'll let you go up for just a little while, if you really think it's your duty.'

'Of course it is,' said Charles.

Elvira smiled at him. 'Then I don't mind,' she said.

Charles regarded her affectionately. 'You're disgraceful, Elvira. You really are,' he said, smiling again.

'But you won't be long, will you?' she asked. 'You'll come down again very soon?'

Charles shrugged his shoulders. 'Well, I shall probably dress for dinner while I'm upstairs,' he told her. 'You can amuse yourself somehow, can't you? You can read the *Tatler* or something.'

'Darling, you don't have to dress for me,' Elvira pointed out, to which he replied, 'It's not for you. I always dress for dinner.'

'What are you going to have for dinner?' she asked. 'I should like to watch you eat something really delicious –'

Charles went to the door. 'Now, be a good girl while I'm away,' he said. 'You can play the gramophone if you like.'

'Thank you, Charles,' Elvira replied demurely.

After Charles had left the room, she got up, looked in the gramophone cupboard, found the record of her favourite song, 'Always', and put it on. She had started to waltz lightly around the room to it, when Edith came in to fetch the tea tray. Hearing the gramophone playing by itself with apparently no one in the room to listen to it, Edith turned it off and put the record back in the cupboard. While the maid was picking up the tray, Elvira took the record out and put it on again. When the song began, Edith gave a shriek, dropped the tray she was carrying and rushed out of the room, while Elvira continued to waltz gaily to the strains of Irving Berlin's melody.

Chapter Eleven

———

Several days later, just after sunset, rain was falling heavily all over Kent. In the living room of the Condomines' house Mrs Bradman, the doctor's wife, was sitting in an armchair, while Ruth Condomine stood by the window drumming on the pane with her fingers. Glancing across at Ruth, Mrs Bradman asked, 'Does the weather show any signs of clearing?'

'No, it's still pouring,' Ruth replied, gazing out of the window at the wet garden.

The doctor's wife continued to look at Ruth. 'I do sympathise with you, really I do,' she said. 'It's been quite a chapter of accidents recently, hasn't it?'

Ruth nodded her head without turning. 'It certainly has been,' she agreed.

'That happens sometimes, you know,' Mrs Bradman told her, obviously hoping to start a conversation. 'Everything seems to go wrong at once – almost as though there were some kind of evil force at work.'

Getting no response to this, she continued garrulously, 'I remember once when George and I went away for a fortnight's holiday, not long after we were married – we were dogged by bad luck from the beginning to end. The weather was absolutely vile, George sprained his ankle, I caught a terrible cold and had to stay in bed for two days – and, to crown everything, the lamp in the sitting room fell over and set fire to the treatise on hyperplasia of the abdominal glands that George had just finished writing.'

'How dreadful,' Ruth murmured absently.

'He had to write it all over again,' Mrs Bradman exclaimed. 'Every single word!'

Ruth, who clearly had been paying no attention to this tale of misery, now turned to face Mrs Bradman and asked, 'You're sure you wouldn't like a cocktail, or some sherry or anything?'

'No, thank you – really not,' the doctor's wife replied. 'It's a little too early for me, I'm afraid, and anyway George will be down in a minute and then we've got to go like lightning.'

She looked at her wristwatch. 'We were supposed to be at the Wilmots' at six,' she said, 'and it's nearly that now.'

Ruth came away from the window. 'Well, I think I'm going to have a little sherry,' she announced. 'I feel I really need it.' She went over to the drinks table and poured a sherry for herself.

Mrs Bradman regarded her sympathetically. 'Don't worry too much about your husband's arm, Mrs Condomine,' she said. 'I'm sure it's only a sprain –'

'It's not his arm I'm worried about,' Ruth replied, but Mrs Bradman, choosing not to react to this, instead continued, 'and I'm sure your maid Edith will be up and about again in a few days.'

Ruth looked at her grimly. 'The latest thing is that my cook gave notice this morning,' she told the doctor's wife.

Mrs Bradman looked shocked. 'Well, really!' she exclaimed. 'Servants are absolutely awful, aren't they? Not a shred of gratitude. At the first sign of trouble, they run out on you – like rats leaving a sinking ship.'

'I can't feel that your simile was entirely fortunate, Mrs Bradman,' Ruth replied with a grimace.

Mrs Bradman looked flustered. 'Oh, I didn't mean that, really I didn't,' she attempted to assure her hostess. 'What I meant was –'

Fortunately, at that moment Dr Bradman came into the room, carrying his medical bag. 'Your husband's arm is nothing to worry about, Mrs Condomine,' he assured her. 'It's only a slight strain.'

'I'm so relieved,' Ruth responded with a polite smile of gratitude.

'He made a great deal of fuss when I examined it,' the doctor went on. 'Men are much worse patients than women, you know – particularly highly strung men like your husband.'

Ruth regarded him quizzically. 'Is he so highly strung, do you think?' she asked.

'Yes, as a matter of fact I wanted to talk to you about that,' the doctor replied. 'I'm afraid he's been overworking lately.'

Ruth frowned. 'Overworking?' she asked, her voice registering disbelief. 'Did he tell you that?'

'No, he didn't, but it's clear to me that he's in rather a nervous condition,' Dr Bradman told her. 'Nothing serious, you understand –'

'What makes you think he's in what you call a nervous condition?' Ruth asked.

'I recognise the symptoms,' he explained. 'Of course, the shock of his fall might have something to do with it, but I would certainly advise a complete rest for a couple of weeks –'

Ruth looked puzzled. 'Do you mean we ought to go away somewhere?' she asked.

'Yes, I do,' the doctor replied. 'In cases like that, a change of atmosphere can work wonders.'

'What symptoms did you notice?' Ruth enquired cautiously.

'Oh, nothing to be unduly alarmed about,' the doctor assured her. 'A certain air of strain – an inability to focus his eyes on the person he is talking to – and a few rather marked irrelevancies in his conversation.'

'I see,' Ruth murmured. When it seemed that the doctor was not going to say anything further, she asked, 'Can you remember any specific example?'

'Well, for one thing,' the doctor replied, 'he suddenly shouted, "What are you doing in the bathroom?" although I wasn't in the bathroom. In fact, I was standing right beside him. And then, a little later, while I was writing him a prescription, he suddenly said, "For God's sake behave yourself!"'

'How extraordinary,' Mrs Bradman exclaimed.

'He often goes on like that,' Ruth told the doctor nervously. 'Particularly when he's immersed in writing a book –'

'Oh, I'm not in the least perturbed about it, really,' Dr Bradman assured her, 'but I do think that a rest and a change would be a very good idea.'

'Thank you so much, doctor,' said Ruth, fervently. Then, gesturing to the drinks table, she asked, 'Would you like some sherry before you go?'

'No, thank you,' he replied. 'We really must be off.'

'Oh, what about our maid?' Ruth remembered to ask. 'How is poor Edith?'

'She'll be all right in a few days,' the doctor told her reassuringly. 'She's still recovering from the concussion.'

'It's funny that both your housemaid and your husband should fall down on the same day, isn't it?' the doctor's wife remarked.

'Yes, if that sort of thing amuses you,' Ruth retorted sharply.

Mrs Bradman giggled nervously. 'Of course, I didn't mean it like that, Mrs Condomine,' she hastened to explain.

'Come along, my dear,' her husband urged her with a rather tight smile. 'You're talking too much, as usual.'

'You are horrid, George,' Mrs Bradman exclaimed, as she rose and went across to Ruth. 'Goodbye, Mrs Condomine,' she said gushingly.

'Goodbye, Mrs Bradman,' Ruth replied as they shook hands.

Dr Bradman now took his turn to shake hands with Ruth. 'I'll pop in and have a look at both patients some time tomorrow morning,' he promised her.

'Thank you so much,' Ruth replied. She was about to add something when Charles came into the room, with his left arm in a sling. Elvira followed him in, invisible, of course, to all but Charles.

Dr Bradman turned to his patient. 'Well, old chap,' he asked, 'how does it feel now?'

'It's all right,' Charles replied unconvincingly.

'It's only a slight sprain, you know,' the doctor assured him.

Charles made a gesture with his left arm in the sling. 'Is this damned thing really essential?' he asked grumpily.

'Perhaps not essential, but it's a wise precaution,' the doctor explained. 'It will prevent you using your left hand except when it's really necessary.'

'Well, I'd intended to drive into Folkestone this evening,' Charles informed him.

'It would be much better if you didn't,' Dr Bradman warned.

'It's extremely inconvenient,' Charles began, only to be interrupted by Ruth. 'You could easily wait and go tomorrow, Charles,' she suggested.

Heard only by Charles, Elvira now added her voice. 'I can't stand another of these dreary evenings at home, Charles,' she complained. 'It'll drive me completely dotty – and, what's more, I haven't seen a movie for seven years, and you promised to take me to the cinema –'

'If you haven't seen a movie for seven years, you're extremely fortunate,' Charles snorted.

'What's that, old man?' the doctor asked him kindly.

Realising that Charles must have been addressing Elvira,

Ruth spoke up. 'Charles, dear,' she said with intense meaning, 'do try to be sensible, I implore you.'

'Sorry – I forgot,' Charles muttered.

'Now, you can drive your car if you promise me that you'll go very slowly and carefully,' Dr Bradman advised. 'Your gear change is on the right, isn't it?'

'Yes, it is,' Charles replied. 'Why do you ask?'

'Well, I want you to use your left hand as little as possible,' the doctor instructed him.

'All right, I'll remember,' Charles nodded.

Ruth looked unhappy. 'You'd be much better off if you stayed at home, Charles,' she suggested.

'Couldn't you, perhaps, drive him in to Folkestone, Mrs Condomine?' the doctor asked her.

'I'm afraid not,' Ruth replied stiffly. 'I have lots to do in the house, and then there's poor Edith to be attended to.'

'Well, I'll leave you to fight it out among yourselves,' the doctor announced. Turning to Charles, he added, 'But remember, if you do insist on driving, carefully does it. Because of the rain, the roads are very slippery at present.'

He turned to his wife. 'Come along, Violet.'

'Goodbye again,' Mrs Bradman said to Ruth, and then, turning to Charles, 'Goodbye, Mr Condomine.'

'Goodbye,' Charles responded, as he showed the Bradmans out of the room.

Ruth, left standing by the fire, spoke intensely to the

apparently empty room. 'You really are infuriating, Elvira,' she said. 'Surely you could wait, and go to the movies another night.'

Elvira's reply was to take a rose out of the vase on the centre table, throw it at Ruth, and run out of the room through the French windows.

Ruth was by now used to seeing objects moving about apparently without aid, at any time of the day or night and in any part of the house or the garden. She picked up the rose and put it back in the vase. Not realising that Elvira had left the room, she said sharply, 'And stop behaving like a schoolgirl. You're old enough to know better.'

At that moment, Charles came back from having seen the Bradmans off the premises. 'What did you say?' he asked Ruth.

'I was talking to Elvira,' Ruth told him.

Charles looked around the room. 'But she isn't here,' he said.

Ruth glared at him. 'Well, she was, a moment ago,' she retorted. 'And what's more, she threw a rose at me.'

Charles laughed. 'She's been very high-spirited all day,' he exclaimed. 'I know this mood of old. It usually meant that she was up to something.'

Ruth regarded him steadily. Then she went to the door, closed it, and came back to Charles. 'You're quite sure she isn't here now?' she asked him.

'Quite sure,' Charles replied, with an indulgent smile.

'Then I want to talk to you,' Ruth said quietly.

Charles looked highly apprehensive. 'Oh, God!' he exclaimed.

'I must, Charles,' she insisted. 'It's important.'

Charles looked at her for a moment without speaking. Then he said, quietly and seriously, 'Ruth, you've behaved very well for the last few days. You're not going to start making scenes again, are you?'

'I resent that air of patronage, Charles,' she snapped. 'I have behaved well, as you call it, because there was nothing else I could do. But I think it only fair to warn you that I offer no guarantee for the future. My patience is being stretched to its uttermost.'

Charles went over to the sofa and sat. 'As far as I can see,' he observed, shaking his head despairingly, 'the position is just as difficult for Elvira as it is for you — if not more so. The poor thing comes back trustingly after all those years in the other world, and what is she faced with? Nothing but brawling and hostility!'

'Poor little thing, indeed. What did she expect?' Ruth asked, belligerently.

'Surely even an ectoplasmic manifestation has the right to expect a little of the milk of human kindness, wouldn't you say?' Charles suggested mildly.

'Milk of human fiddlesticks!' Ruth snapped in reply.

'That just doesn't make sense, dear,' Charles said sweetly.

Ruth came across to the sofa, and leaned over Charles. 'Elvira,' she said slowly and distinctly, 'is about as trusting as a puff-adder –'

Charles looked up at his wife. 'You're like granite, Ruth,' he told her. 'Sheer unyielding granite.'

Ruth ignored this. 'And,' she continued, 'she's a good deal more dangerous than a puff-adder into the bargain.'

'Dangerous?' Charles snorted. 'I've never heard anything so ridiculous. How could a poor, lonely, wistful little spirit like Elvira be in the least dangerous?'

'She could be, quite easily,' Ruth replied. 'And, what's more, she is. She's now beginning to show her hand.'

Charles looked perplexed. 'How do you mean?' he asked. 'In what way is she showing her hand?'

Ruth replied in exasperation, 'For heaven's sake, this is a fight, Charles. A bloody battle. A duel to the death between Elvira and me. Don't you realise that?'

'That's sheer melodramatic hysteria,' Charles told her.

'It isn't melodramatic hysteria,' Ruth insisted. 'It's perfectly true, what I'm saying. Can't you see that?'

'No, I can't,' he answered decisively. 'You're imagining things. You know, Ruth, jealousy causes people to have the most curious delusions.'

Ruth opened her mouth to speak, and then paused. She took a deep breath, and said, quietly but firmly, 'I am making every effort not to lose my temper with you, Charles, but I must say that you are making it increasingly difficult for me.'

'All this talk of battles and duels –' Charles began, but Ruth interrupted him. 'Elvira came here with one purpose, and one purpose only,' she insisted. 'And if you can't see it, then you're an even bigger fool than I thought you were.'

Charles shook his head. 'What purpose could she have had beyond a natural desire to see me again?' he asked, smugly. 'After all, you must remember that she was extremely attached to me, poor child.'

Ruth sighed. 'Elvira's purpose is perfectly obvious,' she replied. 'It is to get you to herself for ever.'

'That's absurd,' Charles retorted. 'Anyway, how could she do that?'

'By killing you off, of course,' Ruth pointed out to him sharply.

Charles looked at her in disbelief. 'Killing me off? You're mad!' he exclaimed.

Ruth paused, and then spoke slowly and meaningfully. 'Why do you suppose Edith fell down the stairs and nearly cracked her skull?' she asked.

'What's Edith got to do with any of this?' Charles sounded thoroughly mystified.

'Edith fell down the stairs because the whole of the top

stair was covered with axle grease,' Ruth told him. 'Cook discovered it afterwards.'

Charles stared at her, unable to believe what he was hearing. 'You're making this up, Ruth –' he began.

'I'm not,' she insisted. 'I swear I'm not.' She went on, in desperation, 'And why do you suppose, when you were lopping that dead branch off the pear tree, the ladder broke? Because it had been practically sawn through on both sides.'

Charles got to his feet. 'But why should she want to kill me? he asked, incredulously. 'I could perhaps understand her wanting to kill you, Ruth, but why me?'

'Because, if you were dead,' Ruth explained to him, 'it would be her final triumph over me. She'd have you with her for ever on her damned astral plane, and I'd be left alive, high and dry.'

When Charles merely gaped at her in astonishment, Ruth continued, 'She's probably planning a sort of spiritual remarriage to you. I wouldn't put anything past her.'

'Ruth!' Charles exclaimed, really shocked at this suggestion.

'Don't you see now?' Ruth asked, aggressively.

Charles still looked shocked. 'She couldn't be so sly – so wicked. She couldn't,' he gasped.

'Couldn't she just?' was Ruth's rhetorical reply.

Charles shook his head in disbelief. 'I grant you that, as a character, she was always rather light and irresponsible,' he admitted, 'but I would never have believed her capable of low cunning, and I don't believe –'

'Perhaps the spirit world has deteriorated her,' Ruth interrupted him.

Charles gazed at his wife. 'Oh Ruth!' he exclaimed miserably.

Ruth addressed him impatiently. 'For heaven's sake, stop looking like a wounded spaniel, and concentrate,' she ordered. 'This is extremely serious.'

'But what are we to do?' Charles asked in desperation.

'To begin with, you're not to let her know that we suspect a thing,' Ruth instructed him. 'You must behave perfectly ordinarily, as though nothing had happened. I'm going to see Madame Arcati immediately. I don't care how cross the old girl is, she's simply got to help us. Even if she can't get rid of Elvira, she must have some technical method of rendering her harmless. If a trance is necessary for that, she shall damn well go into a trance even if I have to beat her into it.'

She looked at her watch, and continued decisively, 'I'll be back in half an hour. Tell Elvira I've gone to see the vicar to ask for his help.'

'This is appalling,' Charles began, but Ruth interrupted immediately. 'Never mind about that,' she ordered him. 'Just remember now, don't give yourself away by so much as the flick of an eyelid –'

At that moment, Elvira came in from the garden, and Charles cried involuntarily to his wife, 'Look out!'

'What?' Ruth asked.

'Er, I merely said it's a nice look-out,' Charles improvised, now that Elvira was close enough to hear him.

Elvira had, indeed, heard him. 'What's a nice look-out?' she wanted to know.

'The weather, Elvira,' Charles told her. 'The thermometer is going down and down. It's positively macabre.'

'I find it difficult to believe that you and Ruth, at this particular moment, can't think of anything more interesting to talk about than the weather,' Elvira replied with a playful smile.

Ruth got to her feet. 'I can't stand this any more,' she exclaimed. 'I really can't.'

'Ruth, dear, please –' Charles looked at his wife pleadingly. But, before he could continue, Elvira enquired mockingly, 'Has she broken out again?'

'Did she say something? What has she said?' Ruth asked Charles.

'She asked if you had broken out again,' Charles told her.

Ruth was incensed. 'How dare you talk like that, Elvira!' she snapped.

'Now then, Ruth –' Charles attempted to silence his wife, but she was now in full flow. 'Charles and I were not talking about the weather, Elvira, as you so shrewdly suspected.' Ruth continued with icy dignity, turning to address Elvira whom she assumed to be now standing in front of her, 'I should loathe you to think that we had any secrets from you.'

Charles motioned to Ruth that Elvira was, in fact, behind her. Turning around, Ruth went on speaking. 'And so I will explain exactly what we were talking about,' she told Elvira.

Elvira immediately ran skittishly to the other side of the room. Oblivious to this, Ruth continued, 'I was trying to persuade Charles not to drive you into Folkestone this evening. It will be bad for his arm, and you can perfectly easily wait until tomorrow. However, as he seems to be determined to place your wishes before mine in everything, I have nothing further to say. I'm sure I hope you both enjoy yourselves.'

With a final glare of fury at Charles, Ruth now swept out of the room, slamming the door behind her.

Chapter Twelve

—▰—

As Ruth stormed out of the room, Charles stood looking at the door in dismay.

'Oh, Charles, have you been beastly to her?' Elvira asked him demurely.

'No, of course I haven't,' Charles replied. 'But Ruth just doesn't like being thwarted – any more than you do.'

Elvira smiled. 'Ruth's a woman of sterling character,' she observed. 'But it's a great pity she's so ungiving – so self-centred.'

Charles frowned. 'As I've told you before,' he said, 'I would rather not discuss Ruth with you. It makes me very uncomfortable.'

'Very well, I shan't mention her again,' Elvira assured him. 'Now then, are you ready?'

Charles looked perplexed. 'Ready for what?' he asked.

'To go to Folkestone, of course,' she reminded him.

Charles now looked extremely uncomfortable. Then, apparently deciding that prevarication was the wisest course to take, he said, 'Well, I want a glass of sherry first, before we set out.'

'You shouldn't drink before you're going to drive,' Elvira told him. Then, with a pout, she continued, 'I don't believe you want to take me to the movies at all.'

'Don't be silly. Of course I want to take you,' Charles insisted, 'but I still think it would be more sensible to wait until tomorrow. It's a filthy night out there.'

Elvira strode across the room, and flung herself into an armchair. 'How familiar this all is,' she muttered crossly.

Charles raised an eyebrow. 'In what way familiar?' he wanted to know.

'All through our married life,' Elvira observed irritably, 'I only had to suggest something, and you would immediately start hedging me off, and telling me that –'

'I'm not hedging you off,' Charles interrupted her. 'I merely said –'

Elvira cut him short. 'All right, all right,' she growled. 'Let's just spend another cosy intimate evening at home, with Ruth sewing away at that hideous table centre or whatever it is she's making, and snapping at us both like a bad-tempered terrier.'

Charles came to the defence of his wife. 'Ruth is perfectly aware that the table centre is hideous,' he informed Elvira in dignified tones. 'It so happens that she intends it to be a birthday present for her mother, who likes –'

'It's no use trying to defend Ruth's taste to me,' Elvira told him dismissively. 'It's thoroughly artsy-craftsy and you know it.'

'It's not artsy-craftsy,' Charles insisted.

Elvira gazed around her. 'The wretched woman's absolutely ruined this room,' she observed. 'Just look at those curtains – and that awful shawl on the piano –'

Charles glanced in the direction of the shawl. 'Lady Mackinley sent that shawl to us from Burma,' he pointed out.

'Obviously because it had been sent to her from Birmingham, and she couldn't stand the sight of it,' Elvira retorted snidely.

Charles approached her. 'If you don't behave yourself, Elvira,' he warned her, 'I shan't take you into Folkestone ever.'

Elvira decided to change her tactics. 'Please, Charles,' she murmured pleadingly, 'please don't be elderly and grand with me. Let's go now – please.'

'Not until I've had my sherry,' he insisted.

'Oh, you are tiresome, darling,' she complained. 'I've been waiting about for hours.'

'Then a few more minutes won't make very much difference,' Charles observed, as he poured himself a sherry.

Elvira flung herself into a chair. 'Oh, very well then,' she agreed petulantly.

'Besides,' Charles added, 'the car won't be back for half an hour at the least.'

Elvira looked startled. 'What do you mean?' she asked sharply.

Charles sipped his sherry nonchalantly before replying, 'Ruth has taken the car. She had to go and see the vicar.'

'What?' Elvira exclaimed, jumping up in extreme agitation.

'What on earth's the matter?' Charles asked her.

'You say *Ruth's* taken the car?' Elvira cried urgently.

'Yes,' Charles replied. 'She wanted to go and see the vicar. But she won't be long.'

Elvira got to her feet, crying, 'Oh, my God! Oh, my God!'

'Elvira! What is it?' Charles enquired anxiously.

'Stop her,' Elvira ordered him. 'You must stop her at once.'

Charles looked puzzled. 'Why? What for?' he asked her.

Elvira jumped up and down frantically. 'Just stop her! Get out and stop her immediately!' she screamed.

'It's too late now,' Charles pointed out. 'She's gone. I heard the car start a few minutes ago.'

Elvira retreated slowly towards the window. 'Oh, oh, oh, oh!' she moaned.

Charles approached her gingerly. 'What are you going on like this for?' he asked, a note of anxiety creeping into his voice. 'Elvira? What have you done?'

Elvira looked extremely frightened. 'Done? I haven't done anything,' she replied unconvincingly.

'Elvira – you're lying,' he accused her.

She backed away from him. 'I'm not lying,' she insisted. 'What on earth is there to lie about?'

'Then what are you in such a state for?' Charles asked her, sounding clearly suspicious.

Elvira was now almost hysterical. 'I'm not in a state,' she screamed, 'I don't know what you mean –'

'You've done something dreadful. I know you have,' Charles insisted.

She backed away from him. 'Don't look at me like that, Charles,' she begged him. 'I haven't done anything – I swear I haven't –'

Charles struck his forehead. 'My God!' he exclaimed. 'The car!'

'No, Charles, no!' Elvira continued to scream.

'Ruth was right,' he shouted at her. 'You did want to kill me. You've done something to the car –'

'Oh, oh, oh, oh!' Elvira continued to howl like a banshee.

Charles stepped towards her. 'What did you do? Answer me!' he insisted.

At that moment the phone rang. Charles went across the

169

room and answered it. 'Hello . . . hello . . . yes, speaking . . . I see . . . the bridge at the bottom of the hill . . . thank you . . . no, I'll come at once.'

He put the receiver down slowly. As he did so, the door to the passageway burst open. Elvira, who was facing the door, began to retreat, walking backwards. 'Well, of all the filthy, low-down tricks!' she yelled. She shielded her head with her hands as she screamed, 'Ow – stop it – Ruth – leave go –'

Still screaming, Elvira ran out of the room, slamming the door behind her. But it opened again immediately, and then slammed shut again, as Charles stared, aghast.

Chapter Thirteen

———

A few days later at about nine o'clock in the evening, Charles Condomine, dressed in deep mourning garb, stood before the fire in the living room, drinking his after-dinner coffee. When he had finished his coffee, he put the cup down on the mantelpiece, lit a cigarette, and settled himself comfortably in an armchair. He adjusted a reading lamp and, with a deep sigh, opened a novel and began to read it. After no more than two or three minutes, there was a ring at the front-door bell. With an exclamation of annoyance, Charles put his book aside, got up, and went out into the hall. Opening the front door, he discovered Madame Arcati standing outside, dressed in the strange, rather barbaric clothing that she had worn on her first visit to the house. Charles invited her in, and led her to the living room.

As he was shutting the living room door, Madame Arcati said, 'I hope you will not consider this an intrusion, Mr Condomine.'

'Not at all,' Charles assured her. 'Please sit down, won't you?'

'Thank you,' she murmured as she took a seat.

'Would you like some coffee?' Charles enquired. 'Or a liqueur, perhaps?'

'No, thank you,' she replied, adding in the same breath, 'I simply had to come, Mr Condomine.'

'Yes?' Charles responded politely.

'Yes, I felt a tremendous urge,' she told him, 'like a rushing wind, and so I hopped on my bike, and here I am.'

'It was very kind of you,' Charles told her with a slight bow.

'No, no, no – not kind at all,' the medium exclaimed. 'It was my duty. I know my duty strongly. I always do.'

'Your duty?' Charles queried, a distinct note of puzzlement in his voice.

She nodded her head vehemently. 'I reproach myself most bitterly, you know,' she informed him.

'Please don't,' Charles assured her. 'There is no necessity for that.' He went to sit in an armchair facing her, and attempted to prepare himself for whatever might be forthcoming.

Madame Arcati came to the point immediately. 'I'm

afraid I allowed myself to get into a huff the other day with your late wife,' she said. 'I rode my bicycle all the way home in the grip of a fierce temper, Mr Condomine, and I have regretted it ever since.'

'My dear Madame Arcati,' Charles began, but the medium held up her hand to stop him from saying anything further. 'Please let me go on,' she urged him. 'Mine is the shame, and mine is the blame. I shall never, never forgive myself. Had I not been so impetuous – had I listened to the cool voice of reason – much might have been averted.'

'You merely told my wife quite distinctly that you were unable to help her,' Charles pointed out sympathetically. 'You were perfectly honest about it. Over and above the original unfortunate mistake – if, indeed, there was any mistake at all – I see no reason for you to reproach yourself.'

Madame Arcati shook her head vigorously. 'No,' she insisted, 'I threw up the sponge. In a moment of crisis I threw up the sponge instead of throwing down the gauntlet, and I –'

'Whatever you threw, down or up, Madame Arcati,' Charles interrupted her, 'I very much fear that nothing could have been done to prevent what happened. It seems that circumstances have been a little too strong for all of us.'

Madame Arcati continued to protest. 'I cannot bring myself to admit defeat so easily,' she exclaimed in angry self-reproach. 'It is gall and wormwood to me. I could have at least concentrated. I could have made an effort, and I *should* have made an effort.'

'Never mind,' said Charles helplessly.

'But I do mind,' the medium insisted. 'I cannot help it. I mind with every fibre of my being.'

She paused, looked around carefully, and then continued, 'I have been thinking a great deal, and I have also been reading up a great deal during the last few dreadful days.' She looked around again, and then asked Charles, 'I gather that we are alone. Am I correct?'

Charles looked around the room before replying. Having satisfied himself that neither of his wives could overhear them, he assured Madame Arcati that they were indeed alone. 'My first wife is not in this room,' he told the medium. 'She is upstairs, lying down. I think the funeral of my second wife exhausted her. I imagine that my second wife is with her, but of course I have no way of knowing for certain. Unlike my first wife, she is not visible to me.'

Madame Arcati looked thoughtful. 'You have not noticed any difference in the – how shall I put it? – the texture of your first wife, since your second wife's accident?' she asked.

'No,' Charles replied. 'Elvira seems much as usual. A little under the weather perhaps, a trifle low-spirited, but that's all.'

The medium's look changed to one of disappointment. 'Well, that washes out that idea,' she observed.

'I'm afraid I don't understand what you mean,' Charles told her.

Madame Arcati shook her head briskly. 'It's just a little theory I had,' she replied. 'You see, in the nineteenth century there was a pretty widespread belief that a ghost who participated in the death of a human being dis-integrated automatically and was made to –'

Charles interrupted her urgently. 'How do you know that Elvira was in any way responsible for Ruth's death?' he queried.

'Elvira,' Madame Arcati repeated. 'Such a pretty name. It has a definite lilt to it, hasn't it?' She hummed for a moment, and then sang softly, 'Elvira, El-vi-ra –'

'You haven't answered my question,' Charles pointed out to her, sounding more than somewhat agitated. 'What makes you think that Elvira had anything to do with Ruth's death?'

Madame Arcati beamed at him. 'It came to me last night, Mr Condomine – it came to me in a blinding flash,' she exclaimed. 'I had just finished my Ovaltine and turned the light out, when I suddenly started up in bed with a loud cry. "Great Scott!" I said, "I've got it!" After that, I began to put two and two together. At three in the morning, with my brain fairly seething, I went to work on my crystal for a little while, but it wasn't very satisfactory – cloudy, you know –'

Charles moved about uneasily. 'I would be very much obliged if you would keep to yourself any theories you may have regarding my wife's death, Madame Arcati,' he told her.

'Of course, of course. My one desire is to help you,' the medium replied immediately. She looked extremely contrite as she continued, 'I feel I have been dreadfully remiss over the whole affair. Indeed, not only remiss but untidy, which from my point of view is almost worse.'

Charles shook his head sadly. 'I'm afraid there is nothing whatever to be done about it now,' he replied. Finding himself close to an armchair, he sat in it.

'But there *is* something to be done,' Madame Arcati exclaimed triumphantly. 'There is!' She produced a piece of paper from her handbag, and brandished it in front of Charles.

'I have found a formula,' she told him. 'Here it is! I copied it out of Edmondson's *Witchcraft and its Byways.*'

'What the hell are you talking about?' Charles asked, irritably.

The medium ignored his tone. 'Pluck up your heart, Mr Condomine,' she encouraged him. 'All is not lost!'

Charles got to his feet. 'Now look here. Madame Arcati –' he began, only to be interrupted by her. 'You are still anxious to dematerialise your first wife, I suppose?' the medium asked.

It was in a lower voice, and with a cautious look towards the door, that Charles replied, 'Well, of course I am. I'm perfectly furious with her, but . . .'

He paused, not certain how to go on.

'But what?' Madame Arcati prompted him.

'Actually,' said Charles, 'Elvira has been very upset for the last few days. You see, apart from me being angry with her, which she always hated even when she was alive, my second wife Ruth has hardly left her side for a moment. You must see that she's been having a pretty bad time, what with one thing and another . . .'

Madame Arcati gave a brisk shake of the head. 'Your delicacy of feeling does you credit,' she complimented him. 'But,' she continued, her tone sharpening considerably, 'I must say, if you will forgive my bluntness, that I think you are a damned fool, Mr Condomine.'

'You are at liberty to think whatever you please,' Charles said stiffly.

'Now, now, now, don't get on your high horse,' the medium admonished him. 'There's no sense in that, is there?' She tapped her handbag. 'I have a formula here that I think will enable you to get rid of her without hurting her feelings in the least. It's extremely simple, and requires nothing more than complete concentration from you, and a minor trance from me. I may even be able to manage it without lying down.'

'Honestly, I would rather –' Charles began. At that moment, the door opened and Elvira came quickly into the room, obviously very upset. 'Charles,' she called to him.

'What on earth's the matter?' he asked her.

Elvira caught sight of Madame Arcati. 'Oh!' she exclaimed. 'What is that wretched woman doing here?'

'She came to offer me her condolences,' Charles lied.

'Oh, really? They should have been congratulations,' Elvira snarled.

'Please don't say that kind of thing, Elvira,' Charles admonished her. 'It is in the worst possible taste.'

He turned to the medium. 'Madame Arcati,' he said, 'please allow me to introduce you to my first wife, Elvira.'

'How do you do, Mrs Condomine?' the medium said politely, looking around and wondering which part of the room she should be addressing.

'What does she want, Charles? Please send her away,' Elvira ordered, walking about the room distractedly.

'In what part of the room is she at the moment?' Madame Arcati asked Charles.

'She's moving about rather rapidly,' he replied. 'I'll tell you when and where she settles down.'

Glaring at the medium, Elvira asked Charles, 'Isn't she the one who got me here in the first place?'

'Yes, she is,' Charles replied helplessly.

'Well, please tell her to get me away again as soon as possible,' Elvira snapped, 'I can't stand this house another minute.'

'Really, Elvira!' Charles exclaimed. 'I'm surprised at you.'

Elvira was nearly in tears as she replied, 'I don't care how surprised you are, I just want to go home. I'm absolutely sick of the whole thing.'

'Now, don't be childish, Elvira,' Charles ordered her. He sounded very annoyed.

'I'm not being childish – I mean it, I really do,' she replied.

Madame Arcati was now by the fireplace, sniffing noisily. 'Very interesting,' she observed, 'Very interesting indeed. I smell ectoplasm strongly!'

'What a disgusting thing to say,' was Elvira's comment on this.

'Where is she now?' the medium asked Charles, who replied, 'She's here, quite close to me.'

Stretching out her hands, Madame Arcati adopted a quasi-mystical tone as she inquired, 'Are you happy, my dear?'

'Tell the silly old bitch to mind her own business,' Elvira shouted, stamping her foot angrily.

Unable, of course, to hear this, Madame Arcati continued to question Elvira, now in a kind of sing-song voice. 'Was the journey here difficult? Are you feeling weary?' she asked the spirit of Charles's first wife.

'She's dotty,' Elvira commented to Charles.

'Just a moment, Madame Arcati,' Charles began to say to the medium, but she was paying no attention to him. 'This is wonderful! Wonderful!' she exclaimed, with her eyes shut tight.

'For God's sake, tell her to go into the other room, Charles,' Elvira requested urgently. 'I've got to talk to you.'

Charles tried again to attract the medium's attention. 'Madame Arcati –' he addressed her, but she stopped him. 'Just a moment, Mr Condomine,' she urged. 'I almost have contact. I can sense the vibrations. Oh, this is magnificent!'

Charles turned to his first wife. 'Oh, go on, Elvira, don't be a spoilsport,' he told her. 'Give Madame Arcati a bit of encouragement.'

'Only if you promise to then get her into the other room,' Elvira replied.

'All right,' said Charles. 'I promise.'

At this, Elvira went across to Madame Arcati and blew gently into her ear.

Madame Arcati jumped for joy. 'Yes, yes! Again, please, again!' she exclaimed.

Elvira blew into her other ear, and asked, 'How's that?'

Clasping and unclasping her hands in a frenzy of excitement, the medium shouted, 'This is first-rate. It really is first-rate. Magnificent. Absolutely stunning!'

'I'm so glad you're pleased,' Charles murmured.

'Charles, you must get rid of her right now. Please!' Elvira begged him. 'Ruth will be here in a minute.'

Charles addressed the medium. 'Madame Arcati,' he said, 'would you think it most frightfully rude if I were to ask you to go into the dining room for a moment or two? My first wife wishes to speak to me alone.'

'Oh, must I?' the medium asked, sounding very disappointed. 'It's so lovely being actually in the room with her. So exciting.'

'It's only for a few minutes,' Charles promised. 'I assure you she'll still be here when you come back.'

'Oh, very well,' the medium agreed reluctantly. 'Just hand me my bag, would you, please? Its on the settee over there.'

It was Elvira who went to the settee, picked up the medium's handbag, and handed it to her.

'Oh, you darling, you little darling!' Madame Arcati exclaimed, blowing a kiss in what she assumed to be the right direction. Then, humming ecstatically, she went off into the dining room, shutting the door behind her.

Chapter Fourteen

———

As soon as Madame Arcati had left the room, Elvira regarded Charles intently and pointed towards the dining room. 'Just how good is that old bag, really?' she asked.

'I really don't know. I've simply no idea,' Charles was forced to admit.

'Do you think she could actually get me back to the spirit world again?' Elvira wanted to know.

'Honestly, my dear child –' Charles began.

'And don't call me your dear child. It sounds so smug and supercilious,' Elvira snapped at him.

'There's no need to be so rude, Elvira,' Charles snapped back at her.

Elvira sighed. 'The whole thing's been a failure – a

miserable, dreary failure,' she moaned. 'And oh, what high hopes I started out with.'

Charles gave a snort of disdain. 'You can't expect much sympathy from me, you know,' he reminded her. 'I am perfectly aware that by far the highest of your high hopes was to murder me.'

'Don't put it like that, Charles,' she complained. 'You make it sound so beastly.'

'It is beastly,' Charles pointed out. 'It's one of the beastliest ideas I've ever encountered in all my life.'

Elvira regarded him sadly. 'I can remember a time,' she said, 'when you'd have welcomed the chance of being with me for ever.'

'Your behaviour has shocked me immeasurably, Elvira,' Charles informed her coldly. 'I had no idea that you could be so unscrupulous.'

Elvira burst into tears. 'Oh, Charles –' she sobbed.

'Oh, for goodness sake, stop crying,' he ordered her.

'They're only ghost tears,' Elvira admitted. 'They don't mean anything, really – but they're still very painful.'

Charles was not in the least sympathetic. 'You've brought all this on yourself, you know,' he told her.

Elvira immediately ceased her crying. 'That's right – rub it in,' she replied angrily. 'Anyhow, it was only because I loved you. The silliest thing I ever did in my whole life was to fall in love with you. You were always unworthy of me.'

'That remark comes perilously close to impertinence, Elvira,' said Charles, whose anger was beginning to rise.

'I sat there, on the other side, just longing for you, day after day,' Elvira told him.

When Charles merely looked at her with disbelief written all over his face, she continued, 'I did. Really, I did. All through your affair with that brassy-looking woman in the south of France I went on loving you and thinking only of you. Then you married Ruth, and even then I forgave you and tried to understand, because all the time I believed, deep down inside, that you really loved me best.'

She paused, momentarily, and then went on. 'That's why I put myself down for a return visit, and I had to fill in all those forms, and wait about in draughty passages for hours on end. If only you'd died before you met Ruth, everything might have been all right. But she's absolutely ruined you. I hadn't been back in the house a day before I realised that. And the books you write aren't a quarter as good as they used to be, either.'

Not surprisingly, Charles was incensed at this. 'That is entirely untrue,' he exclaimed, his voice rising to a shout. 'Ruth always helped me and encouraged me with my work, which is a damned sight more than you ever did.'

'Then that's probably what's wrong with it,' Elvira shouted back at him.

'All you ever thought of,' Charles told her angrily, 'was going to parties and enjoying yourself.'

'Well, why shouldn't I have had fun?' Elvira insisted. 'I died young, didn't I?'

'You needn't have died at all if you hadn't been idiotic enough to go out on the river in foul weather with Guy Henderson and get soaked to the skin,' Charles reminded her.

'So we're back to Guy Henderson again, are we?' Elvira snapped at him.

Charles wagged a finger in her face. 'You know you behaved abominably over Guy Henderson, and it's no use your pretending that you didn't,' he insisted sternly.

Elvira pouted. 'Guy adored me,' she recalled. 'And what's more, he was very attractive. He was a real dish.'

'I distinctly remember you telling me that he didn't attract you in the least,' Charles reminded her angrily.

'Well, you'd have gone through the roof if I'd told you that he did,' she retorted.

Charles glared at her. 'Answer me truthfully now,' he ordered her. 'Did you have an affair with Guy Henderson? Did you or didn't you?' he asked tensely.

'I would rather not discuss it if you don't mind,' Elvira replied with dignity.

'Answer me,' Charles insisted. 'Did you or did you not have an affair with Guy Henderson?'

Elvira smiled enigmatically, before replying calmly, 'No, of course I didn't.'

Charles was not inclined to let the matter rest. 'You let him kiss you though, didn't you?' he asked her, accusingly.

'How could I stop him?' Elvira replied calmly. 'After all, he was bigger than I was.'

Charles looked and sounded furious. 'And you swore to me that nothing happened,' he shouted.

'Of course I did,' she replied, still sounding extremely calm. 'You were always making awful scenes over nothing at all.'

'Nothing at all!' Charles spluttered in exasperation.

'You never loved me a bit, really,' Elvira insisted. 'Not the slightest bit. It was only your beastly vanity.'

Charles took a deep breath. 'Do you seriously believe,' he asked her solemnly, 'that it was only vanity that upset me when you went out in that punt with Guy Henderson?'

Elvira corrected him. 'It was certainly not a punt,' she pointed out. 'It was a little launch.'

'I don't care if it was a three-masted schooner or an ocean liner,' Charles exclaimed in a fury. 'You had no right to go!'

'You seem to forget *why* I went,' Elvira reminded him. 'You seem to forget that you had spent the entire evening making sheep's eyes at the overblown harridan with the false pearls.'

Charles looked shocked. 'A woman in Cynthia Cheviot's position would hardly wear false pearls,' he retorted indignantly.

'They were practically all she was wearing,' Elvira recalled bitchily.

Charles paused before stating, in dignified tones, 'I am pained to observe that seven years in the echoing vaults of eternity have in no way impaired your native vulgarity.'

'That was the remark of an incredibly pompous ass,' Elvira commented, turning away from him.

There was a moment's pregnant silence. Then Charles declared, 'I'm afraid there is nothing to be gained by continuing this discussion.'

Elvira sniggered. 'You always used to say that when you were thoroughly worsted in an argument,' she reminded him.

Charles regarded her with a superior air. 'When I look back on our married years, Elvira,' he informed her, 'I see now, with the most horrid clarity, that they were nothing but a mockery.'

'You invite mockery, Charles,' Elvira retorted swiftly. 'It's something to do with your personality, I think – a certain seedy grandeur.'

Charles looked thoroughly exasperated. 'Once and for all, Elvira –' he began, only to be interrupted by Elvira who was now in full flood of rhetoric. 'You never suspected it, of course,' she declared, 'but I laughed at you steadily, from the altar to the grave. All your ridiculous petty jealousies, and your fussings and fumings –'

Charles shouted her down. 'You were feckless and irresponsible and morally unstable,' he accused her. 'I realised that, even before we left Budleigh Salterton.'

'Nobody but a monumental bore would have thought of having a honeymoon in Budleigh Salterton,' she sneered in reply.

'What's the matter with Budleigh Salterton?' Charles asked indignantly.

Elvira gazed at him in disbelief. 'I was an eager young bride, Charles,' she reminded him. 'I wanted glamour and music and romance. All I got was seven hours every day on a damp golf course, and in the evening a three-piece orchestra playing "Merrie England".'

'It's a great pity you didn't tell me so at the time,' he exclaimed angrily.

'I tried to, but you simply wouldn't listen,' she replied. 'That's why I went out on the moors that day with Captain McGill. I was desperate.'

Charles looked shocked to hear this. 'You swore to me that you'd gone over to see your aunt in Exmouth,' he reminded her.

Elvira shook her head. 'It was the moors,' she repeated.

'With Captain McGill?' he asked, incredulously.

'With Captain McGill,' she affirmed.

Charles erupted in a sudden fury. 'I might have known it,' he shouted. 'What a fool I was. What a blind fool!' He paused before asking her, 'Did he make love to you?'

Elvira sucked her finger and regarded it thoughtfully. 'Of course he did,' she said.

'Oh, Elvira!' Charles exclaimed helplessly.

'But only very discreetly,' she recalled. 'He was in the cavalry, you know.'

Charles took a deep breath. 'Well,' he exclaimed, 'all I can say is that I'm well rid of you.'

Elvira smiled sweetly. 'Unfortunately you're not rid of me,' she reminded him.

'Oh, yes I am,' Charles insisted. 'You're dead, and Ruth's dead. I shall sell this house, lock, stock and barrel, and go away from here.'

'I shall follow you,' Elvira threatened, still smiling sweetly.

'I shall go a long way away,' Charles told her. 'I shall go to South America. You'll hate that. You were always a bad traveller.'

Elvira shrugged her shoulders. 'That can't be helped,' she smiled smugly. 'I shall have to follow you. After all, you called me back.'

'I did not call you back,' he insisted.

'Well, somebody did,' she pointed out. 'And it's hardly likely to have been Ruth.'

'I did not call you back,' Charles repeated. 'Nothing in the world was further from my thoughts.'

'But you were talking about me before dinner that evening,' Elvira declared.

'I might just as easily have been talking about Joan of Arc,' he retorted, 'but that wouldn't necessarily mean that I wanted her to come and live with me.'

Elvira looked thoughtful. 'As a matter of fact, Joan of Arc's rather fun,' she informed him.

'Stick to the point, Elvira,' Charles insisted.

Elvira shook her head. 'When I think of what might have happened if I'd succeeded in getting you to the other world after all – it makes me shudder, it does honestly,' she exclaimed. 'It would have been nothing but bickering and squabbling for ever and ever. I swear I'll be better off with Ruth. At least she'll find her own set of friends and not get in my way.'

'So I get in the way, do I?' Charles asked grimly.

'Only because I was idiotic enough to imagine that you loved me, and I sort of felt sorry for you,' she replied.

Charles gave a sigh. 'I'm sick of these insults,' he told her. 'Please go away.'

'There's nothing I should like better,' Elvira replied. 'I've always believed in cutting my losses. That's why I died.'

'Of all the brazen sophistry –' Charles spluttered.

Elvira interrupted him. 'Call that old girl in again,' she

ordered him. 'Set her to work. I won't tolerate this any longer. I want to go home.' She started to cry.

'For heaven's sake, don't snivel,' Charles snapped at her.

Elvira stamped her foot. 'Call her in right away. She's got to get me out of this.'

'I quite agree,' Charles replied, going to the dining room door and opening it. 'Madame Arcati,' he yelled, 'would you please come in now?'

Chapter Fifteen

———

A moment or two later, Madame Arcati entered the living room, looking about her. 'Is the darling still here?' she asked Charles eagerly.

'Yes, the darling is still here,' he replied grimly.

'Where? Tell me exactly where,' the medium asked, her voice urgent and her eyes darting around the room.

'She's over by the piano – blowing her nose,' Charles told her.

Madame Arcati virtually raced across to the piano. 'My dear, oh, my dear,' she exclaimed and then stopped, words apparently failing her as she beamed at what to her was the empty space in front of her, but what to Charles was the image of Elvira.

'Stop her fawning on me, Charles,' Elvira warned

him, 'or I shall break something. I mean it.'

Charles made an attempt to take control of the situation. 'Elvira and I have discussed the whole business, Madame Arcati,' he announced, 'and she wishes to go home immediately.'

Madame Arcati looked blank. 'Home?' she queried.

'Wherever she came from,' Charles explained. 'You know what I mean.'

The medium looked disappointed to hear this. 'You don't think she would like to stay just a few days longer?' she asked.

When Charles merely glared at her and remained silent, Madame Arcati explained the reason for her request. 'It would be just while I try to get things a little more organised.'

'No, no,' Elvira intervened immediately. 'I want to go right now. This very instant.'

Unable to hear Elvira's voice, Madame Arcati continued to address Charles. 'I could come here and be with her,' she informed him eagerly, 'and I could bring my crystal with me.'

'God forbid!' Elvira exclaimed with urgency.

'I'm afraid not, Madame Arcati,' said Charles. 'Elvira and I are both agreed that she must go as soon as possible. Please strain every nerve, or whatever it is you have to do. Make every effort. You said something about a formula. Can you tell me what it is?'

The medium looked extremely disappointed to hear this. 'Well – if you insist –' she began reluctantly.

'I most emphatically do insist,' Charles interrupted her, at which Elvira began to wail 'Oh, Charles –'

'Shut up!' Charles snapped at Elvira, and then made an apologetic gesture to Madame Arcati to indicate that he had not been addressing her.

Madame Arcati continued to look desolate. 'Well, I can't guarantee anything, you know,' she told Charles. 'I'll do my best, but it may not work. As I said, there's a certain formula –'

'Yes, what is the formula?' Charles asked her immediately.

'It's nothing more than a little verse, really,' she replied. 'It fell into disuse after the seventeenth century.' She paused in thought momentarily, and then added, 'I shall need some pepper and salt.'

'There's pepper and salt in the dining room,' Charles responded quickly before she could change her mind. 'I'll go and get it right away.'

He left the room to do so, and Madame Arcati continued talking, now addressing Elvira on the assumption that she was still standing by the piano – which she was not. 'We ought, of course, to have some Shepherd's Wort and a frog or two,' the medium explained to Elvira, 'but I think I can manage without them. You won't be frightened, dear, will you? It's absolutely painless.'

Charles came back from the dining room with the salt and pepper cruet. 'Will this be enough?' he asked Madame Arcati.

'Oh, yes,' she replied. 'I only need a little. Just put it on the table, please. Now then, let me see –'

Fumbling in her bag, she extracted her spectacles and a piece of paper on which the formula was written.

'Sprinkle the pepper and salt on the table there, will you,' she said to Charles. 'Just a little. Very, very little. There, right in the middle of the table.'

Charles did as he was told, while Elvira commented, 'This is going to be a flop – I can tell you that, here and now.'

Madame Arcati looked around the room. 'Now, would you let me have a few snapdragons out of that vase?' she instructed Charles. 'There's a good chap.'

Charles brought the flowers across. 'Here you are,' he said, as she took them from him and laid them on the table.

Elvira was watching their antics disdainfully. 'Merlin does all this sort of thing at parties,' she observed. 'He bores us all stiff with it.'

'Now then,' Madame Arcati continued, 'We need to have the gramophone playing. In the old days, of course, they used a zither or reed pipes. We'd better have the same record that we had before, I think.'

'I'll get it,' Elvira offered eagerly. She fetched the record, gave it to Madame Arcati and then went over to the mantelpiece to observe the proceedings.

'Well, it's true we have no zithers or reed pipes, so do use whatever you think best, Madame Arcati,' said Charles.

The medium had been watching, fascinated, what had seemed to her to be a gramophone record moving around the room unaided and coming towards her. She grasped it joyfully. 'Oh, if only that Mr Emsworth of the Psychical Research Society could see this – he'd have a fit. He would, really!' she exclaimed in excitement.

Holding the record out in front of her, she said to Elvira, 'Put it on the machine, you little darling,' at which the record was taken from her and floated away from her.

'Don't start it yet, dear,' she called across in the direction of the gramophone, on which the record had appeared to place itself, 'Now then – sit down, please, Mr Condomine. Rest your hands on the table, but don't put your fingers in the pepper. I shall turn out the lights myself.'

She started to go across to the light switch but then stopped, exclaiming, 'Oh, heavens above, I almost forgot!'

Coming back to the table, she made designs in the sprinkled pepper and salt with her forefinger. 'One triangle,' she muttered, consulting her piece of paper. 'One half circle, and one little dot. There!'

'This is a complete waste of time,' Elvira muttered to Charles. 'I tell you, she's an absolute fake.'

'Quiet, Elvira. Anything's worth trying,' he replied, waving her away dismissively.

'I'm as eager for it to succeed as you are, Charles,' Elvira told him. 'Don't make any mistake about that. But I'll lay you ten to one it's a dead failure.'

Madame Arcati was now ready for them. 'If your wife would be kind enough to lie down on the sofa,' she invited, gesturing to the sofa.

'Go on, Elvira,' Charles ordered her.

Elvira went over to the sofa and lay down. 'This is sheer nonsense,' she persisted. 'Don't blame me if I get the giggles.'

'Just concentrate,' Charles instructed her. 'Make your mind a blank. Think of nothing.'

Madame Arcati addressed Elvira, unaware that she was facing that lady's feet instead of her head. 'That's right,' she told her, 'quite right. Hands at the sides, legs extended, breathe steadily . . . one, two . . . one, two.' Turning to Charles, she enquired, 'Is she comfortable?'

'Are you comfortable, Elvira?' Charles asked her.

'No!' was Elvira's terse reply.

'She's quite comfortable,' Charles assured Madame Arcati.

'I shall join you in a moment, Mr Condomine,' the medium told him. 'I may have to go into a slight trance, but if I do, don't pay any attention. Now, first the music, and then away we go!'

She went over to the gramophone, started the record of the song 'Always', and stood quite still by the side of it with her hands behind her head for a few moments. Then suddenly, with great swiftness, she ran to the door and switched out the lights. Her form could now be dimly discerned moving about in the darkness.

Charles gave a loud sneeze. 'Oh dear, Charles. It's the pepper,' Elvira observed, giggling.

'Damn!' muttered Charles.

'Hold on to yourself,' Madame Arcati called to Elvira from the other side of the room. 'Concentrate.'

Walking around the room, Madame Arcati began to recite in a sing-song voice:

'Ghostly spectre, ghoul or fiend,
Never more be thou convened.
Shepherd's Wort and Holy Rite
Banish thee into the night.'

'What a disagreeable little verse,' Elvira exclaimed, at which Charles muttered, 'Be quiet, Elvira.'

Madame Arcati now pulled a chair up to the table and sat opposite Charles. 'Sshh!' she warned him.

There was silence.

'Is there anyone there?' she asked. 'One rap for yes, two for no. Is there anyone there?'

The table gave a loud bump.

'I'm sorry to bother you, Daphne dear,' said Madame Arcati, 'but Mrs Condomine wants to return.'

The table bumped several times very quickly.

'Now then, Daphne,' Madame Arcati went on, 'did you hear what I said?'

After a pause, the table gave one bump.

'Can you help us?' Madame Arcati asked Daphne.

There was another pause, and then the table began to bump violently without stopping.

'Hold on tight, Mr Condomine. It's trying to break away. Oh – oh – oh!' the medium gasped.

The table fell over with a crash. At the same time, Madame Arcati fell off her chair, and the table somehow managed to fall on top of her.

'What's the matter, Madame Arcati?' Charles asked anxiously. 'Are you hurt?'

The medium wailed, 'Oh – oh – oh!' Charles rushed over to the door, turned on the lights, and then ran back to Madame Arcati and knelt over her. 'What on earth's happening?' he asked her.

Madame Arcati was lying on the floor with the table upside down on her back. Charles hurriedly lifted it off. 'Are you hurt, Madame Arcati?' he asked again, shaking her.

Elvira got up from the sofa and came over to look at the

medium, then went to the fireplace. 'She's in one of her damned trances again,' she complained, 'and I'm still here as much as I ever was.'

Charles continued to shake Madame Arcati. 'For God's sake, wake up,' he shouted at her.

'Leave her alone,' said Elvira unsympathetically. 'She's obviously having a whale of a time.'

Madame Arcati began to moan, and Elvira continued, 'If I ever do get back to the spirit world, I'll strangle that bloody little Daphne.'

Suddenly, the medium sat up. 'What happened?' she asked briskly.

'Nothing,' Charles answered her. 'Nothing at all.'

Madame Arcati got up from the floor, while Charles picked up the table and replaced it in its original position.

'Oh, yes, something did happen,' the medium insisted, dusting herself down. 'I know something happened.'

'You fell over – that's all that happened,' Charles informed her.

The medium looked about her. 'Is your wife still here?' she asked, sounding both urgent and anxious.

'Elvira? Of course she is,' was Charles's brusque reply.

Madame Arcati shook her head. 'Something must have gone wrong,' she murmured to herself, sounding perplexed.

'Make her do it properly,' Elvira interjected. 'I'm sick and tired of being messed about like this.'

'Be quiet,' Charles admonished Elvira. 'She's doing her best.'

'Something happened,' Madame Arcati insisted. 'I sensed it in my trance. I felt it. It shivered through me.'

Suddenly, the window curtains blew into the room almost straight, and Ruth walked in. She still wore the brightly coloured costume that she had been wearing on the occasion of her fatal car accident, but her clothes now looked entirely grey. So did her hair and her skin.

Ruth strode over to her husband. 'Once and for all, Charles, what the hell does this mean?' she asked.

Chapter Sixteen

Several hours later, the Condomines' living room was in a
state of extreme disarray. There were birch branches and
evergreens laid on the floor in front of the doors, and crossed
birch branches pinned rather untidily onto the curtains. The
furniture had been moved around and was all over the place.
On the bridge table there was a pile of playing cards, as well
as Madame Arcati's crystal ball, and a Ouija board. Also on
the table were two empty beer mugs and a plate with some
sandwiches still left on it. Madame Arcati was fast asleep on
the sofa, Ruth was leaning on the mantelpiece, Charles sat
perched on the back of the sofa, and Elvira squatted on the
piano stool close to the seance table.

Ruth yawned. 'Well,' she exclaimed, 'we've certainly
done all we can. I must say I couldn't be more exhausted.'

'It must surely be daylight soon,' Elvira observed.

The clock struck five, very slowly. 'That clock has always irritated me,' Ruth complained. 'It looks horrid, and it strikes far too slowly. It's designed to annoy us.'

'It was a wedding present from Uncle Walter,' Charles told her absently.

'Whose Uncle Walter?' she asked.

'Elvira's,' he replied.

Ruth glared at the clock. 'Well, all I can say is he might have chosen something a little less irritating and a little more decorative,' she announced.

'If that really were all you could say, Ruth,' Elvira snapped, 'I'm sure it would be a great comfort to us all.'

Ruth shrugged her shoulders. 'You can be as rude as you like, Elvira,' she told her, grandly. 'I don't mind a bit.' She paused momentarily, before adding, 'As a matter of fact, I should be extremely surprised if you weren't.'

'Oh? Why?' Elvira asked truculently.

'The reply to that is really far too obvious' Ruth replied with a sneer.

'I wish you two would stop all this bickering for one minute,' Charles told them wearily.

Ruth yawned again. 'This is quite definitely one of the most frustrating nights I have ever spent,' she complained.

'The reply to that is pretty obvious, too,' Elvira observed, smiling frostily.

'I'm sure I don't know what you mean,' Ruth exclaimed in great indignation.

'Oh, just skip it,' retorted Elvira dismissively.

Ruth sprang away from the mantelpiece and rushed over to Elvira. 'Now listen to me, Elvira,' she said aggressively. 'If you and I have got to stay together indefinitely in this house – and I must say it's beginning to look unpleasantly likely – we had better come to some sort of arrangement.'

Elvira looked at her cautiously. 'What sort of arrangement?' she asked Ruth.

Before Ruth could reply, Charles interrupted them. 'You're *not* going to stay indefinitely in this house – either of you,' he informed them.

'Well, with you then,' Ruth explained. 'We shall both have to be with you.'

'I don't see why,' Charles replied. 'Why don't you both take a cottage somewhere, and live happily ever after?'

'It was you who called us back, remember,' Ruth told him.

Charles both looked and sounded indignant as he replied, 'I've already explained until I'm black and blue in the face that I did nothing of the sort.'

'But Madame Arcati said you did,' Ruth reminded him.

'Madame Arcati's a muddling old fool,' Charles retorted, with a furious glance at the sleeping medium.

'I could have told you that in the first place,' Elvira sighed.

There was an uncomfortable silence for a few moments, broken by Ruth who announced, 'I do think you're behaving very shabbily, Charles.'

Charles looked aggrieved. 'I don't see what I've done that's so awful,' he complained.

'We have all three of us agreed,' Ruth reminded him, 'that, as Elvira and I are dead, it would be both right and proper for us to dematerialise again as soon as possible. That I admit.'

She paused, and then went on, 'Elvira and I have allowed ourselves to be subjected to the most humiliating hocus-pocus for hours and hours without complaining –'

'Without complaining?' Charles interjected, with a sarcastic edge to his voice.

'We've stood up, we've lain down, we've concentrated,' Ruth continued with determination. 'We've sat interminably while that tiresome old woman recited extremely unflattering verses at us.'

Ruth was clearly in full flow. 'We've endured five seances,' she went on, forcefully. 'We've watched the old cow fling herself in and out of trances until we're dizzy, and at the end of it all we find ourselves exactly where we were at the beginning.'

'Well, it's not my fault –' Charles began to say.

Ruth gave him no chance to continue. 'Be that as it may,' she said, 'the least you could do, Charles, is admit failure gracefully, and try to make the best of it. But your manners are boorish to a degree.'

Charles left the sofa and came over to her. 'I'm just as exhausted as you are,' he pointed out. 'I've had to do all the damned table-rapping, remember.'

'If she can't get us back to the other world, she can't, and that's that,' Ruth stated flatly. 'We shall just have to think of something else.'

Charles groaned. 'She must get you back,' he exclaimed. 'Anything else is quite unthinkable.'

'That's gratitude for you!' Elvira contributed to the exchange.

'Gratitude?' Charles queried, uncomprehendingly.

'Yes,' Elvira replied. 'Gratitude for all the years we've both of us devoted to you. You ought to be ashamed of yourself.'

Charles glared at her. 'What about all the years I've devoted to both of you?' he countered.

Elvira was having none of this. 'Nonsense,' she insisted. 'We've waited on you, hand and foot. Haven't we Ruth? You're exceedingly selfish, and you always were.'

'In that case,' Charles snapped, 'I fail to see why you were both so anxious to get back to me.'

It was only with a supreme effort that Ruth stopped herself from screaming. 'You called us back,' she said, speaking slowly and emphatically. 'You – called – us –

back,' she repeated, 'and you've done nothing except to try to get rid of us ever since we came.'

She turned to Elvira for confirmation of this. 'Hasn't he, Elvira?' she asked.

'He certainly has,' Elvira agreed fervently.

'And now,' Ruth continued, 'owing to your idiotic inefficiency, we find ourselves in the most mortifying position – we are neither fish, flesh nor fowl or whatever it is.'

'Good red herring, that's what we are,' Elvira interjected.

'This can't go on,' Ruth concluded her tirade, glaring angrily at Charles.

'Well, why don't you do something about it?' Charles suggested. 'Why don't you go back to the other world, or whatever you call it, on your own, without prevailing on Madame Arcati to help you?'

'We can't do that,' Ruth told him impatiently. 'You know perfectly well we can't. We simply don't know how to.'

Charles looked at them both helplessly. 'Isn't there anybody on the other side who can help you?' he asked Ruth.

'How the hell do I know?' she replied. 'I've only been there a few days. Ask Elvira.'

Elvira forestalled this. 'I've already told you that wouldn't do any good,' she reminded Ruth. 'Even if we were to get Cagliostro, Mesmer, Merlin, Gil de Retz and the Black Douglas all in a row, they couldn't do a thing. The impetus has got to come from here.'

She paused, and then added mischievously, 'Of course, it may be that perhaps darling Charles does not want us to go quite strongly enough.'

'I certainly do want you both to go,' Charles exclaimed with deep feeling.

'Well, you must have a very weak will, then,' Elvira told him. 'I always suspected that to be the case.'

'It's no use arguing any more,' Ruth declared. Raising her voice, she called out, 'Madame Arcati! Wake up, Madame Arcati!'

'Oh, not another seance,' Elvira groaned. 'Please, not another seance.'

Charles added his voice to Ruth's. 'Please wake up, Madame Arcati,' he implored.

'Why not shake her?' Ruth suggested.

Charles looked dubious. 'No, that might upset her,' he warned.

'I don't care if it bloody well kills her,' Ruth replied viciously.

Charles raised his voice. 'Please wake up, Madame Arcati,' he called again.

The medium awoke, rubbing her eyes. 'What time is it?' she asked, looking around the room.

'It's ten past five in the morning,' Charles informed her, sounding understandably impatient.

She sat up. 'What time did I go off?' she wanted to know.

'Over an hour ago,' Charles replied.

'Curious, very curious,' Madame Arcati observed, reaching for her handbag.

'Forgive me for a moment,' she continued. 'I must just make a note of that for my diary.'

She took a book out of her handbag, scribbled in it, and then asked Charles, 'Are they still here?'

'Yes, they are,' Charles replied, shortly.

The medium looked sad. 'How very disappointing,' she exclaimed.

'It certainly is. Have you any suggestions now?' Charles asked her.

She rose briskly from the sofa. 'We mustn't give up hope,' she counselled. 'Chin up, never give in – that's my motto.'

'This schoolgirl phraseology's driving me mad,' Ruth muttered.

Madame Arcati looked about her. 'Now then –' she began, and then paused.

'Now then, what?' Charles prompted her.

She took a deep breath, and squared her shoulders. 'What do you say we have another seance, and really put our shoulders to the wheel?' she suggested. 'Let's make it a real rouser.'

'For God's sake, not another seance,' Elvira exclaimed, her voice sounding utterly exhausted.

'I might be able to materialise a trumpet if I tried hard enough,' Madame Arcati told Charles. 'That's better than nothing, you know. And I feel as fit as a fiddle after my rest.'

Elvira snorted. 'I don't care if she materialises a whole symphony orchestra,' she said to Charles. 'I implore you not to let her have another seance.'

Charles was inclined to agree with Elvira. 'Don't you think, Madame Arcati, that perhaps we've had enough seances?' he asked her. 'After all, they haven't achieved very much so far, have they?'

Madame Arcati gave him what she clearly intended to be an encouraging look. 'Rome wasn't built in a day, you know, Mr Condomine,' she pointed out.

'I know it wasn't,' Charles admitted, 'but –'

'Well then, cheer up. Away with melancholy!' the medium urged him.

Her chirpy optimism did not convince Charles. 'Now listen, Madame Arcati,' he ordered her. 'Before you go off into any further trances, I really think we ought to discuss the situation a little more.'

This seemed not to disconcert the medium in the slightest. 'Good!' she exclaimed. 'An excellent idea – and while we're doing it I shall have another of these delicious sandwiches. I'm as hungry as a hunter.' She went over to the table and grabbed a sandwich.

'Would you like some more beer to go with it?' Charles asked her.

'No, thank you,' she replied. 'I'd better not.' She munched happily on her sandwich.

'Very well, you're probably right,' Charles agreed, 'but I think I'll help myself to a small whisky and soda.'

Madame Arcati waved her half-eaten sandwich at him cheerfully. 'Make it a double and enjoy yourself,' she exhorted him.

Charles went to the drinks table and mixed himself a whisky and soda, while Ruth muttered, 'One day I intend to give myself the pleasure of telling that old fraud exactly what I think of her.'

'Now, now, she's been doing her best,' Charles admonished his wife.

Hearing Charles's remark, Madame Arcati asked him, 'Are the girls beginning to get despondent?'

'I'm afraid they are, rather,' Charles told her.

Madame Arcati beamed at him. 'Cheer up, we'll win through yet,' she promised. 'Don't be downhearted.'

She went over to sit on the sofa, while Ruth observed nastily, 'If we're not very careful, she'll materialise a complete girls' hockey team.'

'Now then, Mr Condomine,' Madame Arcati addressed Charles. 'Let's have the discussion. Fire away.'

Charles seated himself on a footstool in front of the medium. 'Well, my wives and I have been talking it over,' he informed her, 'and they are both absolutely convinced that it was I who, somehow or other, called them back.'

Madame Arcati nodded her head vigorously. 'That's very natural,' she observed.

'But I am equally convinced that I did not,' Charles insisted.

The medium wagged a finger at him. 'Love is a strong psychic force, Mr Condomine,' she declared. 'It can work untold miracles. A true love can encompass the universe –'

'I'm sure it can,' Charles broke in hastily, 'but I must confess to you frankly that, although my affection for both Elvira and Ruth is of the warmest kind, I cannot truthfully feel that it wold come under the heading that you describe.'

'I should just think not, indeed,' Elvira commented, while Madame Arcati, unable to hear her, told Charles, 'You may not know your own strength, Mr Condomine.'

'I did *not* call them back,' Charles told her firmly. 'Neither consciously, subconsciously, or unconsciously.'

'But, Mr Condomine –' the medium began, only to be cut off by Charles holding up a hand and announcing, 'And that is my final word on the subject.'

212

Madame Arcati looked at him in frustrated silence for a moment, and then said, slowly and clearly, 'Neither of your wives could have appeared, reincarnated, unless there had been somebody – a psychic subject – in this house, who wished for them to come back –'

Charles interrupted her again. 'Well, I assure you it wasn't me,' he said decisively.

'Well, perhaps it was Dr Bradman,' Elvira suggested, giggling. 'And I never knew he cared.'

Responding to Charles's strong assertion of his innocence in the matter, Madame Arcati asked him, 'Are you sure, Mr Condomine? Are you absolutely sure?'

'Absolutely positive,' Charles replied.

Madame Arcati had already selected another sandwich. She was about to take a bite of it, when suddenly she threw the sandwich over her head and got up.

'Great Scott!' she exclaimed energetically, 'I believe I have been barking up the wrong tree.'

'How do you mean?' Charles asked her.

'The Sudbury case!' she shouted enthusiastically.

'I'm afraid I don't understand,' said Charles, looking mystified.

'There's no reason why you should,' Madame Arcati told him. 'It was well before your day.' She stood still, looking extremely thoughtful. 'But I wonder – oh, yes, I wonder –' she began.

'What was the Sudbury case?' Charles asked her. 'I wish you'd explain.'

'It was the case that made me famous, Mr Condomine,' she explained, proudly. 'It was what you might describe in theatrical parlance as my first big smash hit!'

Looking extremely pleased with herself, she continued, 'I had letters from all over the world about it – especially from India!'

'What exactly did you do in the Sudbury case?' Charles asked her, trying not to sound impatient.

Beaming triumphantly, she told him. 'I dematerialised old Lady Sudbury after she'd been firmly entrenched in the family's private chapel, making appearances there for more than seventeen years.'

'But how?' Charles asked urgently. 'Can you remember how you did it?'

'It was pure chance,' the medium admitted, 'an absolute fluke. I happened on it by the merest coincidence.'

'What fluke? What was it exactly?' Charles was impatient to know.

'Wait – all in good time,' Madame Arcati advised. She began to walk about the room. 'Now, let me see,' she exclaimed. 'Who was in the house during our first seance here?'

'Only the Bradmans, Ruth and me, and of course yourself,' Charles reminded her.

Madame Arcati paused. 'Ah, yes, yes, to be sure,' she recalled. 'But the Bradmans weren't here last night, were they?'

'No, of course not,' Charles replied.

'Quickly – my crystal –' Madame Arcati shouted excitedly.

Charles retrieved the medium's crystal ball from the table. 'Here you are,' he said, giving it to her.

She shook the crystal ball furiously. 'Damn the thing, it gives me the pip,' she exclaimed angrily. 'It's gone all cloudy again.'

She looked into it closely. 'Ah! That's better, it's there again. I'm beginning to understand,' she cried.

'I wish I were beginning to understand,' Charles admitted. 'What do you mean? What's there again?'

'A bandage,' Madame Arcati replied. 'A white bandage. Hold on to that. A white bandage.'

Charles looked puzzled. 'But I haven't got a white bandage,' he told her.

'Shhh!' she urged, holding up a hand for silence, while Elvira murmured, 'She's too good, you know. She ought to be in a circus.'

Madame Arcati suddenly ran to the centre of the room, raised her arms, and began to intone:

'Be you in nook or cranny – answer me.
Be you in Still-room or closet – answer me.

Be you behind the panel, above the stairs,
Beneath the eaves, waking or sleeping – answer me!'

Lowering her arms, she said in satisfied tones, 'There! That ought to do it, or I'm a Dutchman.'

'Do what?' Charles asked her, understandably still perplexed.

'Hush,' she cautioned him. 'Just wait.'

She went over to the window and picked up a bunch of garlic, and then went to the writing desk, making cabalistic signs with the garlic as she walked. Next she picked up one of the birch branches and waved it solemnly to and fro.

Ruth got up and approached Charles. 'For God's sake, don't let her throw any more of that garlic about,' she begged him. 'It nearly made me sick last time.'

Charles's attention was still fixed on Madame Arcati. 'Would you like the gramophone on, or the lights out, or anything?' he asked her, in an effort to be helpful.

'No, no,' the medium replied. 'It's near, it's very near –'

'If it's a ghost, I shall scream,' Elvira threatened, while Ruth exclaimed, 'I hope it isn't anybody we know – I shall feel so silly if it is.'

Suddenly, the door to the corridor opened, and the Condomines' maid, Edith, came into the room, wearing a pink flannel dressing gown and bedroom slippers. Her head was bandaged.

Chapter Seventeen

———

Everyone stared at Edith as she came somewhat tentatively into the room. 'Did you ring, sir?' she asked Charles.

Before he could reply, Madame Arcati shouted, 'The bandage! The white bandage!', pointing at Edith's head.

'No, Edith,' Charles told the maid. 'I didn't call you.'

'I'm sorry, sir,' Edith said, sounding confused. 'I could have sworn I heard the bell – or somebody calling. I was asleep . . . I don't rightly know which it was.'

'Come here, child,' Madame Arcati cried excitedly.

'Oh!' Edith gasped, looking anxiously at Charles, who responded by saying to her encouragingly, 'Go on, go to Madame Arcati, Edith – it's quite all right.'

In nervous, faltering steps, Edith approached the medium, who asked her, 'Who do you see in this room, child?'

'Oh, dear,' Edith murmured.

'Answer, please,' Madame Arcati ordered her sternly.

'You, Madame,' Edith began apprehensively, and then stopped.

'Go on,' Madame Arcati urged her.

'The Master,' Edith answered.

'Anyone else?' Madame Arcati asked.

'Oh no, Madame,' Edith said quickly.

'Look again,' Madame Arcati ordered inflexibly.

Edith turned imploringly to Charles. 'I don't understand, sir, I –' she began, only to be interrupted by Madame Arcati ordering brusquely, 'Come, child, don't beat about the bush.'

Elvira strolled over to the fireplace, with Ruth close behind her. Without speaking, Edith followed them with her eyes.

'Do concentrate, Elvira, and keep still,' Ruth murmured to Elvira, who replied in a whisper, 'I can't.'

Madame Arcati, her eyes fixed on Edith, asked her, 'Do you see anyone else now?'

'Oh no, Madame,' Edith replied.

Madame Arcati turned to Charles. 'The girl's lying,' she told him.

'Oh, Madame!' Edith cried, but the medium continued, 'They always do.'

'They?' Charles queried.

Turning back to Edith, Madame Arcati asked her sharply, 'Where are they now?'

'By the fireplace,' Edith answered involuntarily, and then gasped, 'Oh!'

'She can see them,' Charles exclaimed. 'Do you mean she can see them?'

'Probably not very clearly, but enough,' the medium told him.

Edith burst into tears. 'Let me go,' she sobbed. 'I haven't done nothing nor seen nobody. Let me go back to bed.'

'Give her a sandwich,' Madame Arcati suggested, and Charles went to the table to get a sandwich for the maid. 'Here, Edith,' he said, attempting to hand her the plate.

'I don't want a sandwich,' Edith cried, drawing away from him. 'I want to go back to bed.'

'Nonsense!' Madame Arcati exclaimed. 'A big healthy girl like you saying no to a delicious sandwich – I've never heard of such a thing. Now sit down.'

Edith turned to Charles. 'Please, sir, I –' she began.

'Please do as Madame Arcati says, Edith,' Charles told her gently.

Edith sat down. 'I haven't done nothing wrong,' she said, sniffing.

'It's all right,' Charles said, attempting to console her. 'Nobody said you had.'

'If she's been the cause of all this unpleasantness,'

Ruth muttered to Elvira, 'I'll give her a week's notice tomorrow.'

'You might not be here tomorrow,' Elvira answered her with a smirk.

Madame Arcati was still focusing her attention on the maid. 'Look at me, Edith,' she ordered her. When Edith obediently did so, the medium suddenly cried out, 'Cuckoo – cuckoo – cuckoo –'

Edith nearly jumped out of her skin. 'Oh, dear,' she gasped, turning to Charles. 'What's the matter with her? Is she barmy?'

'Here, Edith – this is my finger,' Madame Arcati said, waggling her finger in the maid's face. 'Have you ever seen such a long, long, long finger? Look, now it's on the right, now it's on the left, backwards and forwards it goes – see – very quietly backwards and forwards – tic-toc – tic-toc – tic-toc.'

'The mouse ran up the clock,' Elvira muttered.

'Be quiet,' Ruth admonished her in a whisper. 'You'll ruin everything.'

Madame Arcati whistled a little tune close to Edith's face, and then snapped her fingers. When Edith continued to look stolidly in front of her without flinching, the medium stood back. 'Well, so far so good,' she exclaimed. 'She's off, all right.'

'Off?' Charles queried, puzzled.

'She's a natural,' Madame Arcati told him. 'Just the same as the Sudbury case – it really is the most amusing coincidence.' Rubbing her hands in satisfaction, she continued, 'Now then, would you tell your wives to stand close together, please.'

'Where?' asked Charles.

'Just close to you will be best,' she suggested.

'Elvira – Ruth –' Charles called them.

'I resent being ordered about like this,' Ruth protested, while Elvira complained, 'I don't like this at all. I don't like any of it. I feel peculiar.'

'I'm afraid I must insist,' Charles told them.

'It would serve you right if we flatly refused to do anything at all,' Elvira warned him.

Madame Arcati was already addressing the maid. 'Are you sorry for having been so mischievous, Edith?' she asked.

'Oh, yes, Madame,' Edith replied cheerfully.

'You know what you have to do now, don't you, Edith?' Madame Arcati asked her.

'Oh yes, Madame,' the maid replied.

'I believe it's going to work, whatever it is,' Ruth exclaimed. 'Oh, Charles!' She sounded extremely apprehensive. He gestured to her to be silent, but she murmured, sadly, 'This is goodbye, Charles.'

'Tell that Arcati woman to stop for a moment,' Elvira urged Charles. 'There's something I want to say to you before I go.'

'You should have thought of that sooner,' Charles replied unsympathetically. 'It's too late now.'

'Of all the mean, ungracious –' Elvira began, only to be interrupted urgently by Ruth calling, 'Charles, listen a moment.'

'Lights off!' Madame Arcati shouted in a shrill voice. She rushed to the door herself and switched off the lights. In the dark, Edith began singing 'Always' in a very high cockney voice.

Elvira and Ruth now began to speak simultaneously, in the darkness. 'I saw Captain Bracegirdle again, Charles,' Elvira confessed hurriedly. 'I saw him several times. I went to the Four Hundred with him twice when you were in Nottingham, and I must say I couldn't have enjoyed it more . . .' She went on, her voice fading until her words could no longer be heard.

The same was happening with Ruth. 'Don't think you're getting rid of us quite so easily, my dear,' she began. 'You may not be able to see us but we shall be here all right. I consider that you have behaved atrociously over the whole miserable business, and I should like to say here and now . . .' What she would have liked to say was never heard, for she, too, faded into silence.

'Splendid! Hurrah!' Madame Arcati exclaimed exultantly. 'We've done it!' To Edith, who was still rendering her cockney version of 'Always', she said, 'That's quite enough singing for the moment, Edith.'

Edith stopped singing. After a pause, Charles asked Madame Arcati, 'Shall I put on the lights?'

'No,' she replied. 'I will.' She did so, while Charles went across to the window and pulled the curtains open, allowing daylight to flood into the room. Ruth and Elvira were nowhere to be seen, and Edith was sitting very still on her chair.

Charles glanced around the room cautiously. Then, 'They've gone,' he exclaimed. 'They've really gone.'

Madame Arcati looked pleased with herself. 'Yes,' she agreed. 'I think we've really pulled it off.'

Gesturing at Edith, Charles said, 'You'd better wake her up, hadn't you? Otherwise, she might bring them back again.'

Madame Arcati clapped her hands in Edith's face. 'Wake up, child!' she shouted.

Edith nearly jumped out of the chair, 'Good 'eavens!' she exclaimed. 'Where am I?'

'It's all right, Edith,' her employer assured her. 'You can go back to bed now.'

'Why, it's morning,' Edith observed, looking around her.

'Yes, I know it is,' Charles told her.

'But I was in bed. How did I get down 'ere?' Edith wanted to know.

'I rang, Edith,' Charles lied. 'I rang the bell, and you answered it.' He looked to the medium for support. 'Didn't I, Madame Arcati?'

'Did I drop off?' Edith asked, before Madame Arcati had a chance to reply. 'Do you think it's my concussion again, sir? Oh dear!'

Charles shook his head. 'Off you go, Edith,' he said with a smile, 'and thank you very much.' He pressed a five pound note into her hand, adding 'Thank you very much indeed.'

'Oh, sir, whatever for?' Edith asked. She looked at him in sudden horror. 'Oh, sir!' she gasped, and bolted from the room.

Charles looked surprised. 'What on earth did she mean by that?' he wondered aloud.

'Golly, what a night!' Madame Arcati observed. 'I'm ready to drop in my tracks.'

'Would you like to stay here?' Charles enquired courteously. 'There's the spare room, you know.'

'No, thank you,' she replied. 'Each to his own nest. I'll pedal home in a jiffy. It's only seven miles, you know.'

'I'm deeply grateful to you, Madame Arcati,' Charles told her. 'I don't know what arrangements you generally make, but I trust you will send in your account in due course.'

'Good heavens, no, Mr Condomine,' she exclaimed. 'It was a pleasure. I wouldn't dream of such a thing.'

'But really, I feel that all those trances –' he began.

She cut him short. 'I enjoy them, Mr Condomine. I enjoy them thoroughly,' she assured him. 'I always have, ever since I was a child.'

'Well,' said Charles, 'perhaps you'd give me the pleasure of lunching with me one day soon?'

'Yes, indeed. When you come back. I should be delighted,' she replied.

'Come back?' Charles queried.

Madame Arcati went over to the table and knelt to pick up cards from the floor. Then, straightening up, she lowered her voice. 'Take my advice, Mr Condomine, and go away immediately,' she urged him.

Charles looked suddenly anxious. 'But Madame Arcati,' he asked, 'you surely don't mean that –'

The medium cut in quickly. 'This must be an unhappy house for you,' she explained. 'There must be memories both grave and gay in every corner of it. Also –' She paused.

'Also what?' asked Charles, fearfully.

Thinking better of it, she merely replied, 'There are more things in heaven and earth, Mr Condomine.' She placed her finger to her lips. 'Just go,' she added, softly. 'Pack your traps and go as soon as possible.'

'Do you mean that they may still be here?' Charles asked her, also in lowered tones.

The medium nodded, nonchalantly whistled a little

tune, and then whispered. '*Quien sabe*, as the Spanish say.' She went over to the table to collect her crystal ball, her cards and her Ouija board.

Charles looked furtively around the room. 'I wonder,' he murmured to himself. 'I wonder.' Raising his voice, he said, 'I'll follow your advice, Madame Arcati. Thank you again.'

'Well, goodbye, Mr Condomine,' the medium said cheerfully. 'It's been fascinating, from first to last. Fascinating.' Looking across at the table, she added, 'Do you mind if I take just one more sandwich to munch on my way home?'

'By all means,' Charles assured her, as she got a sandwich from the table on her way to the door. He followed her to see her safely out.

'Don't trouble,' she called back to him, over her shoulder. 'I can find my way. Cheerio once more, and Good Hunting!'

Charles watched her go into the hall, and then came back into the room. He prowled about for a moment as though he were not sure that he was alone, and then called softly, 'Ruth – Elvira – are you there?'

After a pause in which nothing occurred, he called again. 'Ruth – Elvira – I know damn well you're there.' Still getting no reply, he spoke to the apparently empty room. 'I just want to tell you both,' he announced, 'that I'm going away, somewhere where I don't believe you'll be able to follow me. In spite of what Elvira said, I don't think spirits can travel over water.' He paused, and then asked, 'Is that quite clear, my darlings?'

Getting no reply, he went on, 'You said in one of your more acid moments, Ruth, that I had been hag-ridden all my life! How right you were – but now I'm free, Ruth dear, not only of Mother and Elvira and Mrs Winthrop Llewelyn, but free of you too, and I should like to take this farewell opportunity of saying I'm enjoying it immensely –'

Suddenly, the vase on the mantelpiece fell into the hearth-stone and smashed.

Charles laughed. 'Aha – I thought so,' he exclaimed. 'You were very silly, Elvira, to imagine that I didn't know all about you and Captain Bracegirdle – I did. But what *you* didn't know was that I was extremely attached to Paula Westlake at the time!'

The picture above the piano crashed to the floor.

Laughing again, Charles continued, 'I was reasonably faithful to you, Ruth, but I doubt if I would have lasted much longer. You were becoming increasingly domineering, you know, and there's nothing more off-putting than that, is there?'

The clock struck sixteen very quickly.

'Goodbye for the moment, my dears,' Charles called to them. 'I expect we are bound to meet again one day, but until we do I'm going to enjoy myself as I've never enjoyed myself before.'

A sofa cushion flew through the air towards Charles.

'You can break up the house as much as you like,' he announced. 'I'm leaving it, anyhow. Think kindly of me, and send out good thoughts –'

The curtains began pulling up and down, and the gramophone lid kept opening and shutting. The mantel-piece began to shake and tremble as though someone were tugging at it.

'Nice work, Ruth,' Charles observed. 'Get Elvira to help you. Persevere.'

An ornament from above one of the bookshelves fell off onto the floor.

'Goodbye again,' Charles called. 'Parting is such *sweet* sorrow!'

A vase from another bookshelf fell. The curtains fell. The gramophone started playing 'Always' very quickly and loudly. Charles went out of the room, laughing, just as the mantelpiece crashed to the floor and the curtain pole came tumbling down.